"We crossed paths at the bar for a reason," he said to her when they neared what he assumed was her apartment complex.

"I know," she said with a smile. "We are meant to help one another in some capacity. We just have to figure out what capacity that is."

His eyes dropped to her red-colored lips of their own accord. Per usual, they looked appetizing and very suckable.

"You're not going to ask me what flavor I'm wearing?"

Kendrick blinked a couple times. "Uh, flavored what?"

She giggled. "Your mind is in the gutter. I was talking about my lipstick. It's cherry, in case you were wondering."

"I love cherry-flavored anything," he said, his eyes dropping to her lips again.

"Good to know."

They both grew silent again, each staring at the other with a newfound curiosity that Kendrick hoped they'd explore one day. *Kendrick, don't forget that you work together.* He'd had good reason for not dating—or kissing—coworkers, but at the moment, he could care less what that reason was.

Dear Reader,

I'm excited for you to get to know Nicole LeBlanc and Kendrick Burrstone. You originally met Nicole in *Waiting for Summer*. However, what you may find interesting is that Kendrick is the cousin of Imani, Cydney and Lex (the heroines of my Elite Events series).

Both Nicole and Kendrick have been unlucky in love, but it's their unfortunate circumstances that make them more compatible than they think. Sometimes, love finds us when we least expect it, and no matter how hard we try to avoid it, fate always wins in the end.

I hope you enjoy Nicole and Kendrick's Valentine's story as the Bare Sophistication ladies take on Los Angeles, California!

Much love,

Sherelle

authorsherellegreen@gmail.com

Her UNEXPECTED VALENTINE

Sherelle Green

HARLEQUIN® KIMANI™ ROMANCE

Recycling programs
for this product may
not exist in your area.

ISBN-13: 978-1-335-21654-0

Her Unexpected Valentine

Copyright © 2018 by Sherelle Green

Printed in U.S.A.

HARLEQUIN®

www.Harlequin.com

Sherelle Green is a Chicago native with a dynamic imagination and a passion for reading and writing. She enjoys composing emotionally driven stories that are steamy, edgy and touch on real-life issues. Her overall goal is to create relatable and fierce heroines who are flawed just like the strong and sexy heroes who fight so hard to win their hearts. There's no such thing as a perfect person…but when you find that person who is perfect for you, the possibilities are endless. Nothing satisfies her more than writing stories filled with compelling love affairs, multifaceted characters and intriguing relationships.

Books by Sherelle Green

Harlequin Kimani Romance

A Tempting Proposal
If Only for Tonight
Red Velvet Kisses
Beautiful Surrender
Enticing Winter
Wrapped in Red (with Nana Malone)
Falling for Autumn
Waiting for Summer
Nights of Fantasy
A Miami Affair
Her Unexpected Valentine

To my friend Kaysha for inspiring the character of Nicole. One of the things that I've always admired about you is that when you love, you put your all into it. Whether it be friendships or relationships, you are constantly proving that you are someone who lets her heart be her guide. More importantly, you're a great friend and we always have so much fun together. You also have the ability to style your natural hair better than anyone I know. We've known each other for more than fourteen years, and I'm grateful to have you in my life! Thank you for always being a supportive and amazing friend!

Acknowledgments

Thank you to my aunties, Vallerie and Cassandra, for always being there when I need you! As a young girl, I never thought about the fact that my mom's best friends were always at my birthday parties and special events. It wasn't until I reached adulthood that I truly began to appreciate that I had two women in my life who loved me like a niece and would do anything to support my dreams and goals. Auntie Vallerie, you and I are alike in so many ways and oftentimes, I feel like even if no one else understands how I feel, you do! Whether it's a happy dance for no apparent reason or having so much excitement that we can't even go to bed before a fun event, we've always connected on a deeper, emotional level. Auntie Cassandra, I have greatly enjoyed the conversations we've had throughout the years about anything from careers and politics, to food recipes and random news. It's not often that you find someone you can literally talk to about anything under the sun and know that they are as interested in a plethora of topics as you are. You have the unique ability to mix humor with any conversation and I love your positivity.

To two women who mean so much to me, I truly appreciate the love you've given me throughout my life. I don't take it for granted that I can call either one of you at any time and know that you'll be there. That kind of support is priceless!

Chapter 1

"Baby, was that an earthquake I just felt? Because when you looked my way, I swear you rocked my world."

Nicole LeBlanc cringed when the man wearing entirely too much cologne got a little too close to her personal space. She took a step closer to her friend Aaliyah Bai, who was trying to contain her laughter.

"They call me Romeo," the man said as he ran his tongue across his teeth.

"Of course they do," Nicole said sarcastically.

"I bet your lips have been lonely waiting for me to walk across the bar," he continued. "I saw the way you were looking at me."

Nicole rolled her eyes as she downed the rest of her drink. It never ceased to amaze her that the sleaziest of men always seemed to approach her when she was out at a bar. Granted, a bar wasn't the ideal place to find a decent man, but come on. Why did she have to attract the slimy guys?

Nicole turned to face the man. "Listen, buddy, since I'm feeling generous today, I'm going to give you five seconds as opposed to three to get the hell away from me."

"Damn, you're feisty." His eyes brightened, and he placed his unwanted hand on her shoulder. "I can only imagine how you'll be in the bedroom."

Time's up. "You'll never find out," Nicole said as she grabbed his thumb and twisted the way she'd learned in her self-defense classes.

"Shit, baby, that hurts," he whined. Nicole twisted his thumb a little more to prove her point, satisfied when the flirtation left his eyes and was replaced with pain.

"I was just trying to give you a compliment," he said, shaking the hurt from his thumb when she let go. "Females these days are crazy."

When he walked away, Aaliyah finally released the laughter she'd been holding in. "It's only our first night being in LA, and already you've almost brought a grown man to tears. Not sure his horrible idea of flirting was worth you almost breaking his thumb off."

"I didn't apply enough pressure to break off his thumb," Nicole said. "He was just being a wimp. I mean, who calls himself Romeo anyway?"

"Oh, my goodness," Aaliyah said. "Hollywood isn't ready for you."

Nicole smiled as she ordered another drink. "I hope I'm ready for Hollywood."

"You are," Aaliyah said as she placed a hand on Nicole's shoulder. "This is an amazing opportunity for you, and although I'll miss you at Bare Sophistication back in Miami, I'm glad I can visit to help with the pop-up shop in LA."

"Thanks, Aaliyah." Nicole took a sip of her delicious cocktail as she thought about everything that was in store for her over the next couple months. She loved being the lead makeup artist and hairstylist for Miami's Bare Sophistication Boutique and Boudoir Studio in addition to all her freelance work, but now it was finally time to spread her wings.

After making a connection with a television producer who was attending a beauty trade show where she was a vendor, Nicole was given the opportunity to temporarily uproot her life to Hollywood to be the lead makeup artist and hairstylist for a series of Valentine's Day themed commercial ads being filmed. The commercials would all tie together as advertisements for a Valentine's Day documentary about love and relationships. Since the previous makeup artist and hairstylist suddenly quit, Nicole had a lot to prove.

The hardest part about coming to LA was leaving behind her friends and business partners, Summer Dupree-Chase and Danni Allison, owners of Bare Sophistication Miami. Fortunately, the women were very understanding of the opportunity and even better, the ladies decided that Bare Sophistication would have a pop-up shop in LA with an opportunity to do a local commercial for the boutique. Kyra Reed, current assistant manager for the Bare Sophistication Chicago location, would be in LA as well to manage the shop. Nicole would assist with the pop-up when she wasn't filming, while Aaliyah—the Bare Sophistication Miami boudoir photographer—would travel back and forth between Miami and LA to help with the boudoir portion of the business.

Nicole and Aaliyah had arrived in LA hours prior to scope out the location of the pop-up shop and get Nicole settled in her temporary apartment. Her first day on the job didn't officially start for another couple days, and although she'd never say the words out loud, she was nervous about her first major position on a television set.

Aaliyah hopped off her stool. "I'm going to head to the bathroom. Can you order me another mango margarita when the bartender returns?"

Nicole nodded in agreement before returning to her drink. *Just shake off the nerves, LeBlanc. You've got this.* She had no doubt that she'd spend the entire weekend chanting those words to herself.

She ordered Aaliyah's drink and began planning her next few days in her mind. Her thoughts were momentarily interrupted when a man approached and sat in Aaliyah's recently vacated stool.

"Magnificent," she heard him say when he was seated.

Not again, she thought. Aaliyah hadn't even been gone two minutes before another guy decided to hit on her.

"I'm not interested," she said, turning to face him. The man in the sleek navy blue suit looked up from his phone.

"What are you talking about?"

Nicole raised an eyebrow. "I heard you call me magnificent, and although I appreciate the compliment, I'm not interested."

Instead of acknowledging what she just said, he simply stared at her. *Hmm, he is kind of cute.* She wasn't really attracted to the business-suit-and-tie-wearing, clean-cut all-American, but she had to admit that his good looks caught her attention.

"You must be confused," he said. "I was referring to this." He turned his phone to show her an image.

Nicole squinted. "You were referring to a wine bottle?"

"Yes, I was."

Talk about embarrassing. "I'm sorry, I think I misunderstood you."

"There's no thinking needed on this," he said in a monotone voice. "You assumed I was flirting with you and I wasn't. So, you shouldn't have said that you *think* you misunderstood me. You *know* you misunderstood me."

It took all her effort not to let her mouth drop open.

"And it's not just any bottle," he said. "It's a rare 1935 merlot that one can only hope to get their hands on."

"Sounds like one of a kind."

The man gave her a blank stare. "It is." He briefly looked her up and down, and Nicole struggled not to fidget under his stare. "Although I wouldn't expect someone like you to understand," he finally said.

Tonight she'd chosen to wear a pair of high-waisted jeans and a light peach blouse. Her curly dark brown hair was pulled on the top of her head in a high bun, and her jewelry matched her blouse. She knew she looked good, but she also knew that she didn't seem to fit the type of woman Buttoned-up Suit was interested in.

Is this jerk for real? "Excuse me? Where do you get off making assumptions about me?"

"You're one to talk," he said. "Considering you assumed I was flirting with you when I sat down, although I gave you no indication that I was interested."

Nicole was about to give him a piece of her mind when the man stood abruptly after receiving his drink and walked away.

If she'd been back home in Miami, she probably would have told him off even if that meant yelling across the bar. Given that she was new to LA, she felt it best to compose herself.

Maybe I should wait near the bathroom for Aaliyah before I get myself into more trouble. Grabbing her cocktail and the margarita she'd ordered for her friend, she stood and turned to leave only to bump into a solid six-foot-three-inch wall.

"Oh, crap," she said as her feet, encased in peach three-inch pumps, slipped from under her and her drinks went in the air. As she tumbled to the hard-tiled floor of the bar and stumbled to catch her balance, Nicole briefly noticed that the solid six-foot-three-inch wall had a good-looking face and arms to match a deep, throaty voice that was currently warning her to watch her step.

"Shit," he said as part of the liquid in one of the glasses spilled on his white dress shirt. Unfortunately for her, the rest spilled all over her peach blouse.

"Watch out," he said when the second glass dropped from her hand and clacked on the floor. As the music blasted in the background, Nicole thought about those scenes in movies where a damsel in distress stumbled and tried to catch her balance only to be encased by a pair of powerful arms that caught her and pulled her to safety.

When the tall mouthwatering stranger reached out his arms, only to completely miss her outstretched hands, causing her to land even harder on her backside, she realized just how false those movie scenes were.

"Are you okay?" he asked, trying to help her up.

No, sexy guy, I'm not okay. "I'm fine," she said, waving away his hands. She knew she should probably accept his help, but a part of her was too over the events of the night to accept any help. *I must have done something wrong within the past week because karma is not on my side.*

"Oh, God, are you okay?"

She turned to the sound Aaliyah's voice.

"I'm fine, just help me up." She reached for Aaliyah, ignoring the smirk on the man standing next to her. She hadn't even gotten a good look at him, but based off what she'd seen on her journey to landing on her butt, he was delicious. Judging by the wide-eyed look

Aaliyah was giving him, Nicole assumed she'd noticed how attractive he was too.

"I thought you didn't need help," the deep, throaty voice said.

"I meant I didn't need *your* help," Nicole said, using a napkin she had in her back pocket to dab the liquor from her blouse.

Aaliyah cleared her throat. "Really."

Nicole glanced at her, immediately recognizing that motherly tone in Aaliyah's voice. Taking a deep breath, Nicole turned to face the man. When she did, she had to remind herself to breathe. "Thank you for the offer."

"You're welcome." His mouth widened into a full grin. "And I apologize. I wasn't watching where I was going."

Even his pearly white teeth are sexy. "Maybe you should be more careful next time."

"Seriously?" Aaliyah huffed. Nicole just shrugged. Was she coming across a little rude? Yes. Was the sexy guy standing before her making her nervous? Yes. Did she get a little rude when she got nervous? Unfortunately, yes. She either got rude or extremely quiet. Apparently tonight, rudeness won.

Sexy Guy stepped a little closer to her. "If being reckless means I'll run into beautiful women such as yourself, then I'll have to take a pass on being careful."

Oh, he's good. Pickup line or not, she had to admit that she liked how good it felt to hear him say those words.

Nicole crossed her arms over her chest, fully aware that she was probably giving him more of a show than she intended since she'd spilled liquor on her blouse. To his credit, he didn't look down.

"Did you run that line on many women tonight or am I the lucky victim?"

He squinted his eyes before leaning closer to her ear. "I know you don't know me," he said in a low voice. "But I'm not the type of man to waste time running lines on women. You're either interested, or you're not." He lifted his head so that he could look into her eyes. "In case you can't tell, I'm interested, and based off how you were checking me out even as you were in the process of falling, you're interested too. My guess? This whole diva attitude of yours is a way to redirect your attraction so that you don't feel vulnerable."

Nicole sighed. *Sexy Guy: one. Me: zilch.* She wasn't sure if it was the trusting look in his eyes or if the fall on her butt had somehow short-circuited her brain cells, but she found herself smiling at his comment instead of denying it.

"Maybe you should buy her another drink," Aaliyah suggested to the man. She then turned to Nicole. "You should go with him to the bar, and I'll find someone who works here to clean up the mess."

Nicole's eyes grew wide at Aaliyah before she turned to the man. She studied his eyes to see if she saw any hint that he'd rather not buy her a drink.

"Sounds good to me," he said, ending her observation.

She took a deep breath as she turned to walk toward the bar, fully aware that he was close behind her.

"What would you like?" he asked as they sat down on two stools.

"Rum and Coke." If he was going to be sitting this close to her, she needed something stronger than a fruity cocktail.

"So, does Miss Slip 'n Slide have a name?"

Nicole smirked. "Cute."

"I try," he said with a shrug.

I doubt you have to try very hard. He seemed to be one of those men who women just flocked to.

Nicole briefly thought back to their previous interaction to recall if Aaliyah had stated her real name. She was satisfied when she concluded that Aaliyah hadn't.

"It's Bianca," she said, extending her hand. Nicole rarely gave out her real name at bars, no matter how attractive a man was.

"Nice to meet you, Bianca." He accepted her hand. "My friends call me KD."

"Nice to meet you, KD." Nicole couldn't help but glance down at his hand, which was still holding on to hers. *I wonder what the KD stands for?* Even though she assumed it was his initials, the KD made him seem mysterious…edgy.

She immediately missed his hand when he released hers as their drinks arrived. "Are you new to the area?" he asked.

Nicole took a sip of her rum and Coke. "Do I give off a vibe like I'm not from the area?"

"No, you don't. But I frequent this bar, and I've never seen you here before." His eyes quickly roamed her face. As much as she tried to ignore it, her skin heated under his gaze. "And there's no way I would have forgotten a breathtaking beauty like you if you were a regular."

"Here you go with these lines again." Nicole shook her head. "I hope you realize that I'm not going home with you."

"I'm offended," KD said as he placed a hand over his heart. "Can't a man compliment a woman without her assuming he is only giving compliments to get her naked?"

Nicole contemplated his statement. "Point taken. Sorry for assuming."

"Apology accepted," he said as he took a sip of his drink, his eyes trained on hers the entire time. "Besides." He shrugged. "I at least take a woman out on a proper date before getting her naked."

Nicole laughed as KD broke out into a smile. "I appreciate a man with a good sense of humor."

"That's good, because I enjoy making you smile." He leaned closer to her, dropping his voice to a whisper. "Just so you know, I consider this a date."

Her laughter echoed across the bar. He may have been hitting on her, but a man hadn't made her laugh this hard in a while. It helped that he was extremely attractive too. He was wearing gray slacks and a slightly stained white dress shirt—thanks to her liquor spill—minus the tie. To the eye, he appeared to be one of those corporate businessmen who wouldn't know how to have fun if it bit him in the butt. But up close, she saw none of that. The sleeves of his shirt were slightly rolled, revealing a smooth chestnut complexion. His hair was thick, curly and faded on the sides in a way that made her want to run her fingers through it.

As her laughter died, she found him watching her intuitively. She'd just met him and albeit he was still a stranger, she was slightly mesmerized by that look. Although his neatly trimmed goatee accentuated his perfect lips, it was his eyes that gave her pause. They were extremely dark—almost black—and for some reason, she couldn't stop staring at them.

His eyes studied her just as hard, and she wondered what he was thinking about. He opened his mouth to speak when a voice across the room got his attention.

"Bro, we're headed out."

Nicole turned toward the voice and realized it was the same guy from earlier. The one who she'd assumed was hitting on her, only for him to tell her that she wasn't his type.

"That would be my cousin Bryant," KD said. "I was originally coming over to you to apologize for his behavior since I'd overheard how he spoke to you, but we collided instead."

So, the only reason he came over was because of someone else? "It's cool," she said with a shrug as she tried to hide her disappointment. "Consider yourself and your cousin now off the hook."

KD squinted. "Let me rephrase that." He leaned closer. "I came to apologize for my cousin's behavior, but that's not the only reason I came over. I'd noticed you the minute you entered the bar. I already had plans to come over, so I was using Bryant as my excuse. We may share blood, but he's a terrible wingman."

Nicole smiled. "If he was supposed to be your wing-man, then he needs a little work on how to talk to a woman."

"I'm working on it," he said with a smile. "In the meantime, can I get your number and maybe call you sometime?"

Don't forget, girl, you're here for work! Don't get distracted by a guy your first night here. "Sure," she said, ignoring the warning. She rattled off her number as he stood to leave with his cousin and friends.

"I'll be calling you, Miss Slip 'n Slide." His lips cocked to the side in a smile.

"I'll be waiting," Nicole said to herself once he was out of earshot. A quick glance at his butt proved it was probably just as delicious as the rest of his body. *So that's how they breed them here in LA, huh?*

"Earth to Nicole," Aaliyah said as she approached. "If you stare at his ass any longer, you'll strain your neck."

"What did you say?" Nicole asked, turning to face Aaliyah.

Her friend shook her head. "So, I'm guessing your rule about not dating while you were here in LA just went out the window?"

"Girl, please," she said, waving off Aaliyah's state-ment. "Men like KD don't even call like they promise. LA is big, and there are lots of beautiful women here. I'll probably never see him again."

Aaliyah laughed. "I don't know about that. I was watching you guys from the other end of the bar, and he was staring a hole through you. I'm shocked he didn't burn you with the fire in his eyes."

"You're so cheesy." Nicole glanced at the door one more time and was surprised to catch him right before he exited. He nodded in her direction, and she lifted her glass to him.

"I may be cheesy, but I'm also usually right. Mark my words. I bet you'll see him again while you're here."

Deep down, Nicole hoped Aaliyah was right. However, she'd never had luck when it came to men, and she doubted that fact was changing anytime soon.

Chapter 2

"I think we're finally making some leeway with this place," Nicole said, glancing around the room.

"We definitely are," Aaliyah said as she came to stand by Nicole. They'd arrived at the location for the Bare Sophistication Boutique and Boudoir Studio pop-up yesterday morning and were pleased with how much they'd gotten done so far.

"Excuse me," a voice said from the doorway of the shop. "Did anyone order a sexy, somewhat loud and vibrant brown beauty to help run this place?"

Nicole laughed before turning around to face Kyra Reed, the store manager of the pop-up. Kyra was the assistant store manager for Bare Sophistication in Chicago, which was run by her sisters-in-law Winter and Autumn. Although Nicole and Aaliyah worked at the Miami location with the women who oversaw that location—Summer and Danni—employees of the two locations got together twice a year for a sales and marketing summit. Last year, Nicole and Aaliyah had met Kyra, and the three had hit it off immediately. With Aaliyah traveling back and forth between locations and Nicole working on the television commercials and documentary, Kyra would be managing the pop-up day-to-day.

"Hey, lady." Nicole gave her a hug. "We were wondering when you would get here."

"You know how O'Hare airport is," Kyra said. "If you can make it out of Chicago without any delays, then it's a pure miracle."

"Yeah, we get delayed every time we fly out of Chicago," Aaliyah said. "But we figured you were delayed because of that guy you're seeing. When Winter called the Miami office a couple weeks ago, she mentioned that he'd begged you to stay in Chicago and not manage the LA pop-up."

"Oh, he did throw a tantrum," Kyra said. "I told him he was being ridiculous because I'd only be gone for six weeks, and Nicole is only contracted for four weeks to work on the commercials and documentary, right?"

"Right," Nicole agreed.

"So, I told him that after four weeks, I could fly back for a visit before finishing the six weeks."

"What did he say?" Nicole asked.

Kyra rolled her eyes. "That jerk said he didn't think he could be with someone who wouldn't consult him before moving to another state. So, I kindly reminded him that he wasn't important enough to factor into my decision."

"Kyra," Aaliyah said. "Weren't y'all together for eight months?"

"We were. But in that eight months we were only exclusive for three. If he thought three months was enough to trap me, he's sadly mistaken. Anyway," she said with a shrug. "I told him the sex wasn't that good and kicked him out of my apartment."

"That's what I'm talking about," Nicole said, high-fiving Kyra. "Let him know who's boss. These men think women are fine with settling for bad sex when there is good sex waiting to be had."

Aaliyah gave them a blank stare. "How in the world did this turn into a conversation about bad versus good sex?"

Nicole placed a hand on Aaliyah's shoulder. "Girl, you can have all the great conversations in the world, but if he's bad in bed, all bets are off."

"Anyway," Aaliyah said, shaking her head. "Let's try and finish setting up at least half the boutique today since we open in two days, but won't have Nicole's help starting tomorrow."

"That's right," Kyra said. "Miss Big Shot hits the television set tomorrow. I can't wait to hear all about the cute men on set. I heard LA has some good-looking men if you know where to look."

"Didn't you hear?" Aaliyah asked. "Nicole already met an attractive man who spent part of the night at the bar drooling over her."

"He wasn't drooling over me," Nicole said. "It wasn't like that."

"Oh, really?" Aaliyah crossed her arms over her chest. "Tell that to all the women at the bar looking at you with envy and the crushed look on Romeo's face when he saw you talking to KD."

"Is KD the cute guy?" Kyra asked.

Nicole nodded. "Yes."

"And who's Romeo?"

"No one worth mentioning," Nicole said. "And even though KD has my number, I doubt he'll use it. Men like him don't usually call women back."

Kyra squinted in confusion. "Men like what?"

"You know the type." Nicole lifted her hands to demonstrate. "Men who look as good as KD have a flock of women waiting for them to shoot attention their way. Hence, he meets a woman and asks for her number because he enjoys the flirtation and wants a bit of a challenge. Once he's done amusing himself, he goes home, calls one of the many in his herd, and you become the cute woman he met that one night who kept his interest for an hour or two."

"Wow," Kyra said. "You got all that from one bar meeting?"

"Sure did. Knowing what type of man he is from the beginning helps ease the disappointment when he doesn't call. It's easy for men to ask for your number. The difficult part is actually putting forth the effort to pick up your cell and call the number you worked so hard to get the night before."

Kyra and Aaliyah shared a look before Aaliyah

spoke up. "I told Nicole that she shouldn't count KD out. Who knows, she may see him again while she's here."

"I highly doubt it." Nicole clasped her hands together. "Come on, let's finish unloading a few more boxes."

Just as Nicole went to lift a box, her phone vibrated in her back pocket. When she glanced at the text message, her mouth dropped open. "You're shitting me."

Kyra and Aaliyah glanced over her shoulder at the message.

"Is that the guy from last night?" Kyra asked. "The one you just said wouldn't be contacting you?"

"It is. He wants to know if I'm free for dinner tonight."

"Say yes," Aaliyah said. "You know you want to."

I do want to. That's the problem. "I'm supposed to be helping you guys set up the shop."

"We can handle it," Kyra said. "Tell him yes."

While she was still contemplating her response, her phone rang. "Oh, my God, he's calling."

"Answer it!" Aaliyah said.

"And put him on speaker," Kyra said. "You're a terrible flirt, so we'll coach you."

Taking a deep breath, Nicole answered and put the call on speaker. "Hello?"

"Hey, Bianca, it's KD." *Why is his voice so sexy?* Nicole giggled when Aaliyah raised an eyebrow and mouthed *Bianca.*

"Hey, KD. What's up?" Aaliyah quickly put the

phone on mute to tell her friends that she gave KD her middle name as opposed to her first name.

"Nothing much," he said. "I sent you a message, but then remembered that I told you I'd call you last night before I left the bar. I was hoping I could take you to dinner tonight."

Nicole bit her bottom lip as Aaliyah and Kyra mouthed the word *yes*. She unmuted her phone.

"It's kinda last minute," she said, ignoring their eye rolls.

"I know," he replied. "I have a busy week ahead, but I really wanted to take you out on a date. I enjoyed meeting you last night, but our conversation was cut short. I'd love the chance to get to know you more. I could pick you up, as well."

Nicole smiled when she glanced at Aaliyah, who was making a swoon face. *You should just say yes. What's the harm in one date?* "How do I know this is really KD?"

"Seriously," Aaliyah whispered. "What kind of question is that?"

Now it was time for Nicole to roll her eyes at herself. *Oh, how I love that I wasn't blessed with the art of flirting*, she thought sarcastically.

"It's definitely me, Bianca," he said in a deep voice. "And I would love to go out with you."

Okay, enough stalling. "Yeah, I'll go out with you tonight, but there's no need to pick me up. Just let me know where we're having dinner and I'll meet you there."

KD rattled off an address, and she jotted it down in the notes section of her phone.

"I look forward to seeing you tonight," KD said.

"Me, too." She went to end the call and heard him mention her name. "Yes?" she asked.

"I'm sure you assumed I was just like all these other cats out here asking for a beautiful woman's number with no intention of using it, but that's not me," KD said. "This may be too forward, but if there's something I want, I typically go after it."

Nicole swallowed. *What am I supposed to say to that?* "I understand."

"Good." He cleared his throat. "See you tonight."

Nicole disconnected the call and looked at the big smiles on Kyra's and Aaliyah's faces.

"That was almost painful to listen to, but I'm glad you said yes," Aaliyah said.

Kyra nodded. "I agree."

"Even though I'm going on this date with KD, I still refuse to get distracted by a man. It's just one date before I start the journey I came here for. That's it."

"I don't know, Nicole," Kyra said with a smile. "You definitely have to focus on this television opportunity, but KD sounds like the best type of distraction."

Nicole sighed. "He does, right?"

"Yup," Aaliyah said. "But now, we really have to get a lot done before you have to get ready for your date. And no worries, you don't have to tell me that I was right about you seeing him again."

"Whatever," she said with a laugh as she got to work.

Kendrick Burrstone glanced around the semideserted Santa Monica restaurant as he tried to spot Bianca from where he sat at a table on the outside patio.

While most people preferred the hustle and bustle of LA, Kendrick preferred coastal city living. Santa Monica was less than an hour from LA, but they might as well be different worlds.

"Are you ready to order or are you waiting for someone else?"

Kendrick glanced at the waitress. "I'm waiting on someone."

"I'm here," a voice said. Kendrick looked past the waitress to see Bianca walking up in jeans and a sexy black lace crop top. *She looks even better than she did at the bar.* Her curly hair was pulled atop her head in a high bun and she wore little makeup, showcasing the natural beauty of her velvety chocolate complexion. There were so many things about the way she looked that caught his attention, but what really made him adjust himself in his seat were the heeled boots she was wearing.

Kendrick was a sucker for a lady in some sexy shoes, and the strappy heeled boots Bianca was wearing caused his imagination to run wild.

"You look beautiful," he said when she approached. He then stood up and leaned in for a hug.

"Thank you," Bianca said, returning his hug. "You look nice, too." The temperature was a little chillier than what he was used to in California, so he'd chosen to wear a dark gray sweater and jeans.

"Thank you." Remembering that the waitress was at the table, they took a seat and ordered drinks.

"I know Sunday night is a weird time for a date, but I appreciate you accepting."

"It's no biggie," she said. "I needed something to keep my mind off my big day tomorrow."

Kendrick took a sip of his water. "Big presentation?"

"I wish," she said with a laugh. "It's my first day at a new job, and I'm a little nervous."

"Don't be," Kendrick said, shaking his head. "I know we just met, but I'm sure you'll do fine."

"Thanks." The waitress returned with their drinks, and they placed their order for dinner.

"So, let me ask you something," she said. "Was that guy, I believe his name was Bryant, really your cousin?"

"Yeah, he is." Kendrick smiled. "He's not too much of a people person, so myself and some of our friends are often apologizing for things that he says."

She took a sip of her drink, causing Kendrick to advert his eyes from hers to stare at her lips. She was wearing a bright burgundy-colored lipstick, and the color immediately reminded him of red velvet cake.

"What's that look for?" she asked.

He met her eyes. "What look?"

"The one you're giving my mouth right now."

Kendrick laughed harder than he meant to. "Do you always say whatever you're thinking?"

"Pretty much," she said with a smile. "My grandmother always tells me that I don't have a filter. It probably annoys her at times, but it's just how I am."

"I think it's refreshing," Kendrick said. "I appreciate honesty. For me, I'd rather someone keep it real than lie to make me feel better."

"Exactly, but I'm a work in progress," she said. "It's

more difficult to be honest depending on the person. For example, I can be honest with some of my friends, but then I have other friendships that I can't be as honest with. And relationships are the worst, but I'm sure this isn't a topic I should bring up on a first date."

"You can bring up whatever you want around me. There aren't too many topics that I'm not willing to talk about."

"Oh, really." She smiled.

"Can I ask you a question?"

"Sure."

He glanced down at her necklace. "Does your necklace have any meaning behind it?"

"It's actually a crystal." She gently ran her fingers across the stone. "The onyx is good for protection and healing."

"That's interesting," he said. "My mom likes wearing crystals and stones, as well. Did you choose to wear it tonight because it went with your outfit or because you needed to feel the energy from it?"

She opened her mouth to respond just as their food arrived. For a few moments, they ate in comfortable silence.

"A little bit of both."

Kendrick swallowed his food before responding. "What do you mean?"

She glanced at him over the glass of wine she sipped. "I wore this crystal because it matched my outfit, and I also wore it because of its energy. Not that this has anything to do with you, but the last real date I went on was with my ex. Let's just say that the relationship was great in the beginning, but ended horribly. In a way, I guess I'm still healing from it."

"I understand completely," Kendrick said. "My last relationship was full of lies and betrayal. On her end, not mine. I learned some valuable lessons because of that experience."

"Like what?"

Kendrick thought about his relationship with two of his exes. "I learned more lessons than I can even remember right now, but one of the biggest was that I will never date someone I work with."

"I hear you," she said, shaking her head. "I used to work with my ex before I started my own business and partnered with a few friends. Before that, I had to see him all the time. Even worse, it seemed like all the people we worked with were in our business."

"It's a feeling I don't wish on anyone," Kendrick said. "And for me, it's happened more than once, so I now have strict rules against mixing business with pleasure."

She smiled. "Then I guess we should be glad that we don't work together."

"We should," he said with a laugh. "And be thankful I didn't ask to see your résumé to confirm that we never would in the future."

"Can you do hair and makeup?" she asked.

Kendrick shook his head. "I can do my hair, but you don't want me to try and do a makeup tutorial. Are you a graphic or creative designer of any kind?"

"Not at all," she said with a laugh. "I'm not horrible at drawing, but I much prefer to creatively make up faces and eccentric hairstyles than try to design anything."

"Then we're good," Kendrick said, clasping his hands together. "Now we can plan the rest of our lives together without any issues."

She laughed so hard that the waitress came over to ask if everything was okay. In other words, they needed to be quieter so that they wouldn't disturb others who were eating.

Once her laughter died down, she continued eating. Kendrick observed her, wanting to know more about her, but not wanting to seem too nosy. He wasn't sure what it was about her, but she intrigued him more than other women had lately. At times she seemed so transparent, and other times she was hard to interpret.

Conversation through the rest of dinner flowed smoothly. As the night neared its end, Kendrick almost hated to say goodbye, but he needed to get to sleep too. She wasn't the only one with a busy workday ahead.

"Thanks for having dinner with me tonight," he said as they approached her car, which was parked down the street from the restaurant.

"You're welcome." She turned to face him. "Thanks for asking me out."

"It was my pleasure." Kendrick studied her eyes, wondering if a good-night kiss was out of the question since this was their first date. "You mentioned that you're starting a new job, but I'd love to take you out again next weekend if you're free."

Her lips widened into a smile. "I think I'd like that." Her eyes briefly dropped to his lips and had he not been paying attention, he would have missed the longing reflected in her eyes.

He watched the rise and fall of her chest, wanting desperately to see how her lips tasted. *What's the worst that can happen? Just one kiss and I'll be satisfied... at least for tonight.*

Kendrick bent his head toward hers as she stood on her tiptoes, awaiting his kiss. When their lips were centimeters apart, the loud rumble of thunder caused her to jump back from him.

"I forgot it was supposed to rain," he said. "With this drought, all of LA and surrounding areas have been waiting for this storm."

She smiled. "Then I guess we should call it a night." She kissed him on the cheek. "Have a good night, KD."

"You too. I'll call you in a couple days with plans for our next date."

"Sounds good."

Kendrick watched her get into her vehicle just as the first raindrops began to fall. He was still looking in the direction of her car after it was out of sight. It had been more than a year since he'd had such a good and relaxing time with a woman, and whether she knew it yet or not, he planned on seeing a lot more of her.

Chapter 3

"Kendrick, come over here for a second."

Kendrick walked over to where his friends Monty and Angelica were standing. "What's up?" he asked as he approached the group.

"Who do you think is more talented… Viola Davis or Taraji P. Henson?"

Kendrick shook his head. "Another debate?"

"Yeah, man," Monty said. "Ange always thinks she's right."

Angelica smirked. "That's because I usually am."

Monty threw his hands in the air. "See what I mean?"

"I don't know, you guys. They are both amazing actresses."

"We know that, but you have to have an opinion on

it," Monty said. "It's a simple question. Which one is more talented?"

"Kendrick, if you don't answer, Monty will never let me get back to work."

Kendrick laughed, knowing what Angelica said was true. He'd worked with Monty and Angelica in the movie industry for the past six years. They all belonged to The Gilbert Monroe Agency as did most of the crew. Although Kendrick was a creative director, Angelica was a visual effects editor and Monty was a cameraman, they were lucky enough to have been placed on several projects together.

Most recently, they'd each specifically been requested by a major client to do a series of Valentine's Day commercials that would tie into the promotion of a documentary on the true meaning of love.

"I guess if I had to answer, both are fierce and leaving a mark in Hollywood."

Monty sighed. "That's not an answer, Kendrick."

"Well, it's the best one I got."

A voice sounded on the intercom. "Meeting in ten in the main galley."

"Let's go now and make sure we get a seat," Angelica said. Kendrick couldn't help but be excited for this meeting since he was itching to get back on set. He hadn't worked on a commercial since before the Christmas holiday.

Whenever he had too much free time on his hands, he tended to do something reckless. And by reckless, he meant he had a tendency to occupy his time with the wrong type of women.

But Bianca was definitely the right type of woman. She was funny, beautiful, had a great—yet edgy—personality. However, she wasn't the type of woman he needed to see again. Kendrick had made a vow to focus solely on his career in hopes of landing a director role before the fall. He didn't have time to date around, especially a woman like Bianca.

Unfortunately, he doubted he could stay away from her. She was the type of woman he always imagined he could be with. He'd been immediately drawn to her when he met her at the bar, and their date last night exceeded his expectations. He realized that he was getting more attached than he probably should.

Another date won't hurt. Although he didn't have any time to seriously date, he couldn't pass up the opportunity to get to know her more. One could argue that he was thinking too much about the situation, but he'd have to disagree. If anything, he wasn't thinking enough given all he'd been through with women in the past couple years.

"Look, I spot some seats." Kendrick followed Angelica and Monty to three open seats in the corner of the room.

"Hey, you never did tell me why you missed poker night yesterday," Monty said.

"I wasn't aware that I had to give you a rundown of my schedule when I cancel," Kendrick said with a laugh. "But if you must know, I had a date."

Angelica rolled her eyes. "An actual date or a booty call?"

"An actual date." Kendrick smiled as he thought

about the flushed look on Bianca's face last night when they'd almost kissed.

"I'd say it was a very good date given that smile on your face," Angelica said. "What about all your non-dating rules and avoiding love until you land a lead director role?"

"I still plan on sticking to my plan. A few harmless dates won't hurt."

"A few?" Monty asked. "One date and you're already planning on seeing her again? This isn't the Kendrick I know."

"Very funny." Kendrick shrugged. "I don't know, man. It's something about her that's different. She has this no bullshit attitude that's kinda refreshing. She says whatever is on her mind without caring what others may think."

"You got all this from one date?" Angelica asked.

"Well, technically we hung out the first night we met, so I guess it's more like two dates."

"Two dates and Mr. Dodge Cupid's Arrow is already planning on more dates." Angelica gave Monty a knowing look. "Monty, I think working on these Valentine's Day commercials is going to his head."

"It's not that big of a deal," he said. "I'm just open to enjoying the company of a woman, that's all. Nothing serious."

"So, I take it she doesn't work in the industry?" Monty asked. If there were any two people who worked in television who knew the drama he'd gone through with his ex, it was his two friends Monty and Angelica.

"She didn't say what she did specifically, but I know

it has to do with makeup and hair because she mentioned enjoying making up faces and designing hairstyles."

Angelica lifted an eyebrow. "And you didn't ask to see her résumé just to be sure?"

"I actually said she was lucky that I didn't ask for it," Kendrick said with a laugh. "So, no, I didn't ask. Guys, I'm better than I used to be. Bianca and I just enjoyed one another as two people would on any first date. Nothing more."

"Except that you want to see her again," Monty said.

"Which says a lot, considering your past," Angelica added. Voices in the front of the room interrupted their conversation.

"As much as I enjoy meeting up with women in my black book, it feels nice to go on a date again," Kendrick whispered. "And this is LA, so the fact that she's not from here and not in the television or film industry is a good thing."

"Okay, everyone," the producer said to the crew gathered in the packed room. "As most of you know, we're running behind schedule with filming the commercials. Valentine's Day is right around the corner, so we only have four weeks to finish shooting the remainder of the Valentine's Day commercials and documentary to get them out before the holiday. That is not a lot of time, so be prepared to work overtime."

Movement on the right side of the room got his attention as someone slid through the door, but too many people were standing for him to see who it was.

"Thank you for all your hard work so far on both

projects, and now I'd like to introduce you to the new members of our team who will be filling in for the crew we lost to other projects."

As the producer introduced the new set design team, Kendrick's eyes were glued to the backside of a woman who felt vaguely familiar. The next moments seemed to happen in slow motion as the woman was introduced to the group, her gaze finding his as she glanced around the room. The widening of her eyes proved she was just as surprised to see him as he was to see her.

The next few minutes of the meeting flew by so quickly that Kendrick didn't notice the woman was already headed his way until she was standing in front of him.

"Hey, KD," she said when she approached. "You work in television?"

He didn't answer until Angelica nudged him. "Um, yeah," he finally said. "I have for six years."

"Oh," she said when he didn't say more. "Today's my first day in the industry."

Of course it is, because the universe had a funny way of making him pay for his past booty calls.

"Hi, I'm Angelica Smith and this is Monty Williams."

"Nice to meet you," she said. "I'm Nicole LeBlanc."

"Nicole?" Kendrick's eyes studied hers. "You told me your name was Bianca."

She gave a sheepish grin. "Actually, Nicole is my first name. When we met at the bar the other day, I didn't know you so I gave you my middle name. I guess I should have corrected you yesterday."

"So, you lied?" Kendrick said, a little harsher than he'd planned.

"It wasn't like that," she said. "How we met was awkward enough. Back where I'm from, women don't just give out their name to strangers until they know a little more about them."

"And where exactly are you from?"

She frowned. "I'm from Miami, but I'm not sure I want to answer any more of your questions based off the accusatory tone in your voice. What gives, KD?"

"KD?" Angelica questioned. When he glanced at his friends, he caught that parental look in their eyes. Angelica and Monty were only a few years older than him, but they never failed to remind him of that fact.

"I guess I can't get on you about your name when I didn't give you my full name either," he said. "KD is short for Kendrick Dominic and my last name is Burrstone. Some call me KD, but most call me Kendrick."

Her eyes softened. "Guess that makes us even." She extended a hand. "It's nice to officially meet you, Kendrick."

"It's nice to meet you too, Nicole," he said, accepting her handshake. "I missed part of your introduction. What's your role on set?"

She smiled. "I'm the new makeup artist and hairstylist for the commercials and documentary."

"Congratulations," he said. "Based off our conversation last night, I'm sure you'll do well."

She studied his eyes. "Thanks, Kendrick, I appreciate that."

He didn't miss the soft way his named rolled off

her tongue. Even under the circumstances, he still felt the chemistry between them. Just a few minutes ago, he'd been convinced he'd see her again, but now? Now, those thoughts went out the window.

He was uncomfortable. She could tell. And he wasn't the only one. Her morning had already started off rocky when she realized that she'd misplaced her lucky crystal necklace and run out of her favorite lipstick. To top it off, she'd taken the wrong train into work and was almost late for her introduction meeting.

The last person she expected to run into at her new place of employment was KD—or Kendrick, as she'd just learned. The only thing more awkward than spotting Kendrick in the audience during her introduction was speaking to him while trying to ignore the look of surprise and frustration on his face.

The surprise she could understand. But the frustration? She didn't know what that was about.

She glanced at his friends before setting her eyes on him. "Well, it was nice seeing you again, but I'm going to head over to check out my station."

"Okay," he said. "It was nice seeing you too."

She squinted her eyes before turning to walk away. *I mean, do I smell or something? He can barely face me. What happened to the man I went on a date with last night?*

"I'll walk with you," said the woman who'd introduced herself as Angelica.

"Thanks."

"Have you gotten a tour?" Angelica asked when they were out of earshot of the men.

"Not yet, but I believe the producer's assistant said she'd give me a tour in an hour or so."

"Which basically means you'll never get a tour," Angelica said with a laugh. "We're behind on shooting, so it's all hands on deck right now."

"No worries," Nicole said. "I planned on setting up my station anyway. The assistant pointed me in the right direction when I arrived. Granted, we were walking fast to make the meeting on time, but I think I got the idea."

"I'll take you to it just in case."

Nicole followed Angelica, annoyed that her mind was still stuck on Kendrick. *What's his deal anyway?* Did she imagine that he was into her as much as she thought he was? He seemed so forthcoming last night and that night at the bar. But today? Today he seemed like he rather be doing anything other than talking to her.

"Don't take it personally," Angelica said, interrupting her thoughts. "Kendrick can be a real sourpuss when he gets his hopes up about something only to have it thrown back in his face."

"What did he get his hopes up about?"

Angelica smiled. "You."

"Me?"

"Yeah, you. Before the meeting started he was telling us how much he liked you."

Nicole frowned. "He sure has a funny way of showing it."

"Ignore him," Angelica said, waving her arms in the air. "Seeing you here just caught him off guard. He'll get over it eventually. Kendrick is just really particular with separating his personal and professional lives."

Suddenly, a memory of what he'd said from last night popped into her mind. *I have strict rules against mixing business with pleasure.* Duh, of course! She didn't know why she hadn't remembered earlier.

"He was caught off guard because he doesn't date people he works with, and as of today, him and I work together."

"Bingo," Angelica said as she placed her pointer finger in the air. "Kendrick is my friend and all, but the guy is a stickler for rules. And by you being here, my dear, it puts him in jeopardy of breaking one of his biggest."

"This is crazy," Nicole said, shaking her head. "We only went on one official date. The least he could do is be cordial to me. I mean, will we even cross paths that much? What's his role here anyway?"

"He's the creative director," Angelica said. "And you're right, you both won't work too closely together, but your paths will definitely cross. Like I said before, we're all hands on deck right now. Here you are." Angelica pointed to a slightly ajar door. "Your station will be here, but I assume you'll be on set when filming for touch-ups on hair and makeup. The producer or his assistant will probably be by soon to give you more details."

"Thanks, Angelica," Nicole said. "It was much easier finding this place with assistance."

"You're welcome. If you need anything else, don't hesitate to reach out."

Once Nicole was in the room by herself, she sat in the high styling chair and stared at her reflection in the mirror. *This is your day*, she reminded herself. *It's the most high-profile job you've ever had, and the worst thing you can do is focus on a man.*

She knew her warning was much needed, but even so, she couldn't stop thinking about Kendrick. It was one thing when she was trying to remind herself not to think about a man when she was in the confines of her own solo space. It was another thing entirely when she'd have to see the object of her desire every day when he wasn't interested in her anymore. *This should be interesting.*

Chapter 4

"And cut. Folks, that's a wrap for this commercial. Let's set the stage for the next one. Filming will begin tomorrow morning."

"Good job, Nick," Kendrick said to the director after Nick had given instructions to the crew for tomorrow.

"Thanks, man. You too."

As he had been doing for the past four days, the minute Kendrick was out of his chair, he headed to his right and out the side door. Typically, he would chat with Angelica, Monty and some of the other crew. However, since he had to see Nicole every time she came on set to touch up makeup for the actors and actresses, he'd gotten out of there.

Unfortunately, today was also the day that Angelica decided to intervene with his new routine.

"Oh, no, you don't," she said, following him. "Tonight a few members of the crew are going to the bowling alley down the street. You have to come."

"I have plans tonight."

Angelica placed a hand on her hip. "Plans with who?"

"Bryant," he said, thinking quick on his feet. Anyone else who he normally hung out with lately was part of the crew that he assumed was going bowling.

"That's funny," Angelica said, waving her iPhone in front of Kendrick. "Because I texted Bryant a little while ago, and he said you didn't have plans with him tonight."

Kendrick shook his head. "I should have never introduced Bryant to you and Monty."

"Kendrick, you are putting forth so much effort to avoid Nicole. Don't you think that is a little silly? Monty and I really like her, and so does most of the crew."

"I'm not avoiding her."

Angelica quirked an eyebrow. "Oh, really? Is that why you've slipped out this side door every day?"

He shrugged. "I have things to do."

"Liar. It doesn't matter anyway because you have to go. The production manager isn't going and said you'd buy a round of drinks for everyone."

"The assistant director isn't going?"

"Nope! Neither are any of the producers, so you can stop thinking about the hierarchy of who else could cover a round of drinks because…it's you…and you're coming. So, man up! Most the crew is there and the rest of us are headed out soon."

She's right, man, he thought after Angelica went back inside. *You're acting ridiculous.* He definitely wasn't behaving like a thirty-five-year-old man, but more like a teenager who was avoiding a woman he had a crush on for fear that he wouldn't be able to hide his attraction.

Mind made up, Kendrick went back inside to join the remaining crew headed to the bowling alley.

"Men against women," someone yelled as they put on their bowling shoes.

"Game on," another yelled. Nicole laughed at the smack talk going on around her. The television crew had blocked off two lanes at a local bowling alley, and she was honored when Angelica and Monty had invited her to join them.

She was almost finished with her first week with the crew. Although leading the makeup and hairstyles for the commercials and ensuring the actors and actresses were camera-ready had been going amazingly well, she'd been making a conscious effort to be more of an extrovert.

It wasn't that Nicole didn't like meeting new people, but oftentimes, she was a little awkward around new people. It was something she'd been working on for years and had only recently gotten better at.

"Ladies, our team captain has finally arrived," Monty said to the group. Nicole glanced up after she finished tying her shoes. *Kendrick.* She'd seen him on and off set all week, but he'd barely made eye contact with her since they'd started working together.

As he dapped fists and exchanged hugs with the crew, Nicole took the time to observe him in a way she hadn't been able to all week. He was wearing dark jeans and a beige long-sleeved button-up that would look simple on any other man, but not Kendrick. On Kendrick, the simple outfit looked a lot better than it should.

She didn't think it was possible, but he looked even sexier than he had the first night they'd met. And apparently, a lot of the women in the crew felt the same way. She'd walked in on several conversations in the kitchenette of women discussing how great Kendrick looked in his rugged, yet classic, style. Or how easy he was to talk to about their man problems, and that his advice was extremely helpful. It seemed that everyone liked being around Kendrick, and he was friends with most of the crew. *Except me...* Her feelings would probably be more hurt if another reoccurring topic people discussed about Kendrick wasn't the fact that he strict rules about dating anyone in the television and film industry. Apparently, quite a few women had tried to get him to change that rule and failed. So instead of being the guy every woman set their sights on dating, every woman aimed to at least maintain a friendship with him. Too bad she couldn't get anything past a "hello" or "goodbye."

"Are you doing okay?" Angelica asked as she approached.

"Yeah, I'm doing good. Thanks for inviting me."

"Anytime," Angelica said. "Do you like bowling?"

"Actually, I'm pretty good at it. I was in a bowling league in high school and college. Even a little after college before I decided to focus on my career. I have my own bowling ball and shoes, but I left them back home in Miami."

"You're a bowler," Angelica said enthusiastically. "As in, you were in leagues and therefore really great at it?"

Nicole squinted her eyes. "Um, yeah. I guess that's what I'm saying."

Angelica rose from her seat. "Don't be so confident, boys." She pulled Nicole from her seat so fast that she almost tripped over one of her shoes that she'd just changed from. "We have a semipro on our hands. Nicole is going to be our team captain, and I hope you know that you're going down!"

"Oh, no no no no," Nicole stammered. "I'm not a semipro. Not even close. Don't get me wrong, I'm a good bowler, but I don't need to be team captain."

"Relax," Angelica said. "This is all in fun and games, but if you must know, the women have lost to the men the past three times we've bowled, and they won't let us forget it. I'm not trying to pressure you, but we could use a win or at the least give them a run for their money."

Nicole followed Angelica to where the other women were standing. They all looked at Nicole expectantly.

"Okay," Nicole said with a sigh. "I'll be team captain, but first we need to strategize the order we list the players."

Angelica gave her a wide-eyed stare. "Picking the order of players takes strategy?"

"Yes, it does. For example, we may want a mid-level bowler to go first to start us off right. Then our weaker players in the middle. Our closers—meaning those who bowl well—will be at the end. So, who's on what level?"

Nicole glanced around at the other women, who were wearing the same look on their faces as Angelica.

"Okay," Angelica said. "I'm midlevel, so I'll go first. And you're our pro, so you go last." The other women nodded in agreement.

"Okay, that works. Does anyone know how to throw a good hook?" Nicole asked.

"I do," said Britt, one of the writers for the commercial series. "I take self-defense classes, and one of the first things they teach you is how to throw a good left or right hook."

Nicole laughed. "I meant a bowling hook. It's a technique you use to bowl the ball."

"Oh," Britt said in disappointment. "I can't even throw a curve ball. I once tried and ended up knocking down pins two lanes over."

"No worries. Anyone else have any bowling skills?"

Each woman sheepishly looked to the floor. Although Nicole took her bowling games seriously, all she could do was laugh. She was sure it sounded like she was speaking a foreign language.

"We'll make it work," Nicole said. "Before we start, I'll give each of you a few pointers." She couldn't turn them into good bowlers in ten minutes, but she could at least teach them the basics.

She's beating me, Kendrick thought as he waited for Nicole to bowl on her lane before he took his turn on his. Even though she was beating him only by fifteen points, she was still winning, and that fact only made him more intrigued.

"Staring at my ass isn't going to help you bowl better," Nicole said with her back still to him. The laugh he released was so loud, he was sure he drew the attention of the rest of the crew. Hell, he and Nicole were practically the entire show since they were the only true bowlers on both teams.

"I beg to differ," he said, ignoring the warning bells he'd been hearing all week when it came to Nicole. "I think staring at your ass will definitely help me bowl better."

She glanced at him over her shoulder with a sneaky smirk on her face. They were on the seventh frame, and both were the last to bowl on each team. Until now, they had been shooting discreet glances at each other, but neither had voiced anything aloud. As they neared the end of the game, it seemed all bets were off.

"Try not to look," she said quietly so only he could hear. He would have asked her what she meant by that, only he found out seconds later when she bent over a little farther than necessary, giving him a great view of her butt in her jeans. He shouldn't have been staring, but he was a man, after all, and when a man saw a nice ass, he looked. Period.

"Your turn," she said after bowling a strike. She unzipped the crop jacket she'd been wearing, revealing her tight tank and beautiful round breasts. *Shit.* He knew she had a pair of delicious breasts, but he had yet to see them on display the way they were now. He didn't even have to look back at the other men to see if they were admiring her figure, as well.

That wasn't the only thing that caught his attention. Nicole had three visible tattoos, one of which was on her breast.

"That's it, girl. Show him what you're working with," Angelica yelled from her seat. Nicole laughed, the sound tickling his ears in the best way. Despite her best attempt to distract him, he bowled a strike.

"She's still ahead," Monty whispered when he and Nicole were almost up again. "You have to find a way to distract her because she's only hitting strikes and spares."

Kendrick glanced at Nicole and caught her staring at him. She raised her drink, obviously satisfied with the fact that she was beating him. *Damn, she even looks good sitting there doing nothing.* Her curls were pulled up on both sides and flowing down her back in the middle. The curly Mohawk style fitted her personality and tonight she was sporting a bright purple lipstick that matched a design in the jacket she had taken off. Kendrick had never really paid attention to lip colors before, but Nicole's lips commanded his undivided attention.

When Monty announced that it was time for them to go, Kendrick had a thought. *If she likes tats, maybe it's time I show off a couple of mine.* One thing Kendrick rarely did was show off his tats in a work setting. However, this was technically a gathering of friends he happened to work with. Besides, he'd been to a pool party with a few of them before, so it wasn't anything they hadn't seen.

Before he stepped up to the lane, he removed his button-up, leaving him in a white short-sleeved tee. May not seem like much, but he had a couple tattoos that were known to get a lot of attention, especially from others in the tattoo community. Just as he'd predicted, Nicole's eyes roamed over his arms in admiration.

Kendrick stepped up to the lane and bowled another spare, so his only hope in catching up to Nicole was if she didn't bowl a strike or spare. He turned around in time to catch her biting her lower lip as she continued to observe him. *Got her,* he thought as he walked toward her.

Leaning close to her ear, he lowered his voice. "Try not to drool too hard, sweetie. You wouldn't want to slip and fall when you take your turn."

"Boy, please," she said, slapping his arm. "You're not all that."

"Oh, really, I'm not?" He met her eyes. "Because just a few seconds ago, you were undressing me with your eyes. Unless I imagined it, you bit your bottom lip in a way that proved you liked what you saw."

"I bit my lip because I was contemplating my next move, not because I was admiring you. I'm surprised you didn't trip over that big ego when you took your turn."

Instead of responding, his eyes dropped to her lips. "That color looks nice on you. Some women can't pull off bright lipstick, but you make it look sexy."

She gasped, apparently caught off guard by the compliment. "Uh, thanks. It's one of my favorites."

He lifted her chin, bringing her lips closer to his eyes. "I can see why. It's hard not to stare at your lips when they look so delicious. Reminds me of cotton candy."

"That's funny," she said, a little breathless. "Because this happens to be flavored lipstick and the flavor is cotton candy."

Crap. Time to backpeddle. "You shouldn't have said that."

She smirked. "You shouldn't be standing this close."

"You shouldn't have given me a reason to be this close." His hand dropped from her chin.

"You shouldn't have been checking out my ass or my chest."

His eyes briefly dropped to her breasts. "You shouldn't be wearing those jeans or a shirt cut so low if you didn't want me to look. But you know what I think?"

"What do you think?" She crossed her arms over her chest, then dropped them to the sides when she saw his eyes drift there again.

"I think you remembered what I said at dinner last weekend about not dating people I work with and decided that you'd test my restraint by flirting with me without saying anything."

Her eyes widened. "As I said during dinner, I understand your rule about not dating people you work with. And for your information, I don't flirt. I've never been good at it."

"I don't believe that," Kendrick said, shaking his head. "You've been doing a damn good job all night."

"That's maybe because I know we'll never go there."

"Go where?" he asked.

"You know what, never mind." She picked up her bowling ball. "It's time for me to bowl."

Kendrick lifted his hands in a way to let her know he wasn't going to stop her anymore. He didn't miss the last glance she gave of the tats on his arms before she bowled.

"It's a split," Monty yelled after Nicole had bowled her first ball.

"There's no way you're getting that," Kendrick challenged. "Be prepared to lose your lead."

When Nicole looked his way, she exuded confidence. "Watch me work," she said before bowling the perfect hook and landing a spare.

"Damn," Monty said. "There's only two more frames left. We're going to lose to the women, and they will be gloating for weeks."

"You're damn right," Angelica said with a laugh. Nicole brushed past him with a look of satisfaction on her face.

"Don't worry, Kendrick. Next time, I'll try to go

easy on you so I don't embarrass you in front of your friends and completely whoop that ass."

Kendrick quirked an eyebrow. "Is that so?"

Instead of responding, she just smiled and joined the other ladies. After the last frame, Nicole had beaten Kendrick by twenty-one points and secured the women's win.

"Man, how could you have let them win?" Monty asked. "We always beat the women."

"Nicole's on their team now, so we better get used to more competitive games."

"Now I have to clean Angelica's condo after work for an entire week."

Kendrick laughed. "That's what you get for always making bets with her. Even if it wasn't bowling, you always lose to her. Wouldn't it be easier to just tell her how you feel instead of losing all the time?"

"I don't know, man," Monty said with a shrug. "Angelica is used to dating those actor types who have starring roles in action movies. She's not going to date a cameraman."

"You never know unless you tell her how you feel. You can't be afraid of entering a relationship with her based off what-ifs. Yeah, it may not work out, but what if it did? What if you miss out on something good because you were scared to make a move and take a chance?"

Monty stood up from his seat and turned Kendrick's body toward where Nicole sat unlacing her bowling shoes and laughing at something Angelica said. "Seems to me like you need to be taking your own advice,"

Monty said. "A lot of the guys like Nicole, and if you don't make a move, someone else will."

Kendrick spent a few more seconds observing Nicole before he began removing his bowling shoes, as well. Monty may have had a point, but Kendrick wasn't sure it was a good idea. *Remember what happened last time, man. You can't afford a repeat of that. Too much is at stake this time.* As long as he remembered what he'd gone through with his ex, he'd keep things in perspective.

But Nicole isn't Veronica or Amanda. Maybe you need to date a woman like her instead of letting your past relationships define how you handle the future.

After all these years, Kendrick had learned that it was easy to let past relationships affect future relationships. The hard part was learning from that lesson and not letting it define your future. He was still working on the latter.

Chapter 5

"I'm all about experiencing new things, but I think it's strange to have to do speed dating with people you work with. Don't you agree?" Angelica asked.

Nicole laughed. Angelica had been complaining about the mock speed-dating event since they found out about it on Friday morning. Now they were waiting for the client to arrive and explain what he wanted them to do.

"I agree, it does seem a bit unethical to have any single employees on the television crew participate in speed dating, but it's what the company that's hosting the charity event wants, so we have to oblige, right?"

"I guess so," Angelica said. "But I still don't like the idea."

On Friday and Saturday mornings, the crew successfully recorded one of the short commercials, so they had only four more left, plus the documentary. Instead of a day off on Sunday as the production team had promised, all single crew members were asked to meet at the location where a speed dating charity event would be held the weekend before Valentine's Day to match dates for the holiday. The goal of the mock speed dating was to give the crew a better idea of how it would work so that they could better advertise and shoot the commercial.

To Nicole, it seemed to be overkill since speed dating wasn't rocket science, but it's what the client wanted, and what the client wanted, the client got.

"Does your annoyance with this have anything to do with Monty?" Nicole asked.

Angelica frowned. "No, why would it?"

"I don't know," Nicole said as she raised her shoulders. "I just assumed that you two were dating or something based off how much you flirt with one another."

"No way," Angelica said with an awkward laugh. "Monty and I are just friends. We both married young and divorced young. Now we're nearing our forties and finally able to live life on our own terms. We bonded over our divorce stories and he, Kendrick and I joined The Gilbert Monroe Agency at the same time, so we're close friends. That's it."

"If you say so." Nicole observed Angelica, who— as she expected—was looking at Monty. "I guess I like teasing you about Monty because of the way he looks at you. He thinks he's being discreet, but it's obvious to me."

"Really?" Angelica asked. "How does he look at me?"

Nicole lowered her voice so no one would hear except Angelica. "Every time you come into a room, his eyes light up. And he's always picking an argument with you or starting a debate because I think he genuinely likes you so badly, he doesn't care what you guys talk about, as long as you're talking. Let's not forget about the times when he watches you with this longing look in his eyes when he thinks no one is looking. I'm sure if I see it, others do too."

"I didn't know he looks at me like that. I guess I don't pay attention because I try my best not to look at him in that same way."

Nicole's eyebrows rose. "So, you do like Monty?"

"That's not what I meant," Angelica said, shaking her head. "I meant that since we're friends, I just stare at him as one friend would another. As a pal. Like two close friends who care about each other in a friendly way. Like a man and his dog. Or a woman and her favorite pair of shoes."

Nicole rolled her eyes as Angelica continued with her thoughts, which didn't make any sense. "Angelica," Nicole said, stopping her rant, "I didn't mean to get you worked up. All I meant to do was tell you that although I can tell that you like Monty as *more* than a friend, I'm pretty sure he likes you just as much, if not more."

"You think so?" she asked in a perky voice.

"Yes." Nicole laughed. "I bet he's staring at you right now." Angelica glanced in Monty's direction and blushed. "I'll take that as a yes."

"Maybe you're right," Angelica said. At Nicole's upturned eyebrow, she changed her statement. "Okay, so you're definitely right. I like him and I'm pretty sure he likes me, but I think we're both just scared to jump into a serious relationship after our divorces. And judging by the way you and Kendrick are around each other, I have a feeling you understand how we feel."

"Kendrick and I aren't the same as you and Monty. We met up a couple times before I started working with the agency, but he'd never date someone he works with. He mentioned his last relationship being filled with lies and betrayal, but I wish I knew exactly what happened."

Angelica's face grew serious. "It's not my place to share that story, but he does have his reasons. Even so, I'm pretty sure he likes you and doesn't know how to handle the fact that you both work together."

"We only work together until Valentine's Day," Nicole said. "After that, I will go back to freelancing and working at a lingerie boutique and studio just like I was before this."

"You're talented," Angelica said. "The Gilbert Monroe Agency doesn't pass up on talent. Kendrick's probably thinking they may ask you to join the agency full-time after this project is completed."

"You think so? I never even thought that was a possibility."

"It's definitely a possibility." Angelica glanced at Kendrick. "I've only known Kendrick for six years, but he's gone through a lot. He's stubborn, so just give him time and I'm sure he'll come around."

Nicole glanced at Kendrick and caught him staring

at her with a look she couldn't quite place. *Interest? Intrigue? Longing?* She quickly adverted her eyes to avoid analyzing him just as the client walked in the room.

"Ladies and gentlemen, I want to thank you all for joining us today for a mock speed-dating event. Today's participants will only include your television crew, and there's about thirty of you here. We want to get started by assigning numbers. My assistant is walking around and passing out numbers to each of you. Although you all know one another, the numbers are how you will refer to a dater. She is also passing around a survey that you will have to fill out for every person you speak with today.

"And please don't worry. These results will be confidential. It's just to give you an idea of how this works. But unlike when we do the real event the weekend before Valentine's Day, we won't actually be matching anyone. Also, women will each be stationed at their own small table, so the men will rotate. Last but not least, have fun with this!"

"See," Nicole said to Angelica. "He said have fun, so let's go have some fun!" Angelica didn't look convinced.

This is not fun, Nicole thought, now that she'd spoken to four men. She figured that doing this event with people she knew—even for a week—was better than participating with strangers. She'd been prepared to at the very least have casual conversation and get to know her coworkers better. Unfortunately, the men seemed to have something else in mind.

"So, what's your idea of a wild night?" David, one of the cameramen, asked. "Skinny-dipping in a pool or skinny-dipping in the ocean?"

Someone save me. "The choices are so different, I can't imagine only choosing one," she said sarcastically.

"I know, right?" David said. "I think both would be pretty awesome. Especially if you and I try them both together. Maybe sometime after work this week?"

Nicole dropped her head to the table. "This can't be real life," she said.

"Are you okay?" David asked. "If you prefer to skinny-dip in a lake, I can make that happen too."

Nicole lifted her head. "I will never skinny-dip with you, David. Furthermore, I would never go on a date with you either."

He frowned. "That's a harsh thing to say. Maybe we should change the topic. What's your favorite sexual position?"

"Oh, hell, no." Nicole shook her head. "Is it time to change partners yet?" she asked to whomever was on the planning team and within earshot. Luckily, the announcement was made mere seconds before David began talking about sex.

Nicole breathed a sigh of relief that she wasn't forced to curse out a coworker in front of the present crew members, until she realized Kendrick was next up to sit at her table. When he sat down, all relief went out the window.

"Hi," she said.

"Hey." Unlike David, Kendrick had a killer smile. He was so attractive, it was intoxicating. *Get yourself together, LeBlanc. No need to be nervous.*

"Are you okay?" he asked.

"Why do you ask?"

"I heard David's questions to you," Kendrick said. "Pretty forward."

"And so off base if he thinks I would ever go for him," Nicole said. "I thought he was cool until our conversation."

"Maybe our conversation can turn this around," he said with a lopsided grin. "First question, have you lived in Miami all your life?"

"For the most part, yes," she replied. "I was raised by my grandparents. What about you? Have you only lived in LA?"

"No," he said. "I was raised by my mother, and her family is from Chicago. I lived in Chicago until my senior year of high school."

"Why did you and your mom move to LA?"

Kendrick adjusted himself in his seat. "She landed an opportunity here, and I was headed down a reckless path in Chicago. She thought it would be good for me to finish out high school in California."

"Was it a good decision?"

"The best," he said. "I wouldn't be where I am today without my mom. Another question. You said you lived in Miami for the most part. What other places have you lived?"

"I've lived in Texas, Virginia, Germany and China."

"Wow," he said. "That's a lot of places."

"It is," she said as she thought about each place. "But Miami has always been where I call home. Do you consider Chicago or LA home?"

"Right now, I consider LA home, but I consider Chicago where I'm from since it's the place I grew up and I was born and raised there. Most of my family— cousins, aunts, uncles, grandfather—still live there."

"I've been to Chicago on a quick work trip before," Nicole said. "I know a couple women who live there and own a lingerie boutique. I work for the Miami location and we opened a pop-up in LA while I'm here. The woman managing that is also from Chicago."

Kendrick squinted. "I know of a lingerie boutique in Chicago, but I can't remember the name."

"Is it Bare Sophistication?"

"That's it," he said, snapping his fingers. "A few of my cousins are the owners of Elite Events Incorporated, and they are friends with the owners of Bare Sophistication. The Dupree sisters, right? I think I met Winter and Autumn at my cousin Lex's wedding when she married Micah Madden. He's—"

"He's Winter and Autumn's cousin," Nicole finished. "I know him too. I've also briefly met your cousins before, but we didn't get to talk much. My friend Kyra knows them well and she always talks about how great they are."

"They are pretty great," Kendrick said with a smile. "I'm proud of them."

"I'm sure they're proud of you too," she said. His smile slightly faltered. "Did I say something wrong?"

"No, you didn't," he said, meeting her eyes. She couldn't be sure, but it seemed as if he wanted to say more, but wasn't sure if he should.

"Last question," he said after a few seconds. "Have you ever felt like even though you have close family and friends who are there for you and care about you, you can never truly be yourself? Or worse, being yourself doesn't fit the vision they have of you in their minds?"

Nicole glanced away at the truth behind his questions. "I've felt that way my entire life," she said, reflecting on times she'd rather not think about. "It's strange to be the only person who thinks the way you do or speaks the way you do. Feelings that others want you to explain, but you can't."

"They don't get it," Kendrick said. "Folks always want you to have an explanation for why you behave a certain way or speak a certain way, but sometimes, things can't be explained." He fidgeted with the edge of the heart-shaped tablecloth. "And holidays like these just remind those who are lonely, just how lonely we actually are."

We? Is he trying to tell me he's lonely? Based off what he'd said, it didn't seem far from the truth. "That's true," she said. "But Valentine's Day isn't only about the love you share with someone you're dating. It can be about family and friends sharing love, as well."

Kendrick smirked. "Don't tell me you're one of those 'Valentine's Day is the most romantic holiday' kind of women?"

"Not exactly," she said. "It's not that I'm a fan of

Valentine's Day, but I am a fan of love and the idea of showing love to anyone in your life who you care about."

Kendrick observed her. "Was there ever a time in your life when you opened your heart to love and the feeling wasn't reciprocated?"

"Too many times to count," Nicole said with a sigh. "I guess, by all accords, when I think about the rejection I've faced from a loved one, you'd think I wouldn't believe in love at all. But it's quite the opposite."

Kendrick leaned a little closer. "You believe in love even more, don't you?"

"It's more like I desire love because I don't feel like I've ever truly had it except from a handful of people."

"I value your point of view," Kendrick said. "I wish I had your optimism on love. For me, it's hard to be that vulnerable around someone. Being vulnerable only opens up you to heartache."

"Although I agree with you," she said, her voice softer than before, "some may say this conversation we're having is a topic that leaves us exposed to our vulnerabilities. So, I'd say you're doing a good job at opening up your heart to me."

Kendrick leaned back and ran his long fingers over his face. "That's the problem, Ms. LeBlanc." His eyes met hers. "Whenever I'm around you, I can't seem to stop myself from opening up and wanting to learn more about you. Have you always had this effect on men?"

Never... "I can't say that I have. I spent my twenties searching for someone who would understand me the way that you explained, and in the end, I lost myself in the process. Now that I'm thirty-three, I finally realize that loving myself is the most important thing, and every day I work toward that goal."

They sat there for a couple minutes in silence, each lost in their own thoughts. The sound of the bell to switch daters woke them from their trance.

"That was a long round," Kendrick said.

"No, it wasn't," Monty replied as he approached the table. "You both talked for two rounds. Since you were so engrossed in your conversation, we skipped you."

"I didn't even realize," Kendrick said as he stood. Before he sat at the next table, he looked at her over his shoulder and smiled. *Yup, I'm a goner.*

"I'm not as suave as Kendrick, but I've been known to charm a woman or two." Monty made a motion of flipping his hair over his shoulder. "Either that or they entertained me because I was funny to look at."

Nicole laughed when Monty winked at her. "I needed that laugh."

"I figured." Monty sat straighter in his chair. "So, do you want to talk or do you want me to tell you the embarrassing thing that Kendrick did the first day we officially met."

"Embarrassing moment, please."

"I was hoping you'd say that." Monty's voice got lower. "It all started when we were on set of our first commercial."

A minute into the conversation, Nicole was laughing so hard, tears streamed from her eyes.

Chapter 6

"Welcome to Bare Sophistication," Nicole said when she heard someone walk into the boutique.

"Did anyone order a sassy aunt to kick off this shindig?"

"Aunt Sarah," Aaliyah screamed. "I'm so glad you're here."

"My sweet girl," Aunt Sarah said as she pulled in Aaliyah for a hug. "How was your flight?"

"It was okay," Aaliyah said. "I landed late last night, and we've been prepping all morning."

It was Wednesday night, and the pop-up shop had been doing well. It seemed that Bare Sophistication was finding its own sweet spot in LA. This evening, they had decided to throw a party to introduce the boudoir studio. Nicole would be offering makeup tutorials all night, and Aaliyah would be taking photos. Kyra would manage the floor with the two employees they'd hired. The goal was to book at least fifteen appointments for the weekend before Aaliyah went back to Miami.

"Okay, what can I do to help?" Aunt Sarah asked after Aaliyah had introduced her to Kyra.

"Follow us," Nicole said. "The studio is in the back, and we need quite a bit of help." Nicole and Kyra had been so busy getting the boutique together, they'd waited until the last minute to organize the studio.

"The furniture is all here, but we have to get the rugs down first, set up the appetizers and wine. We also have to set up the booking table so that we can take appointments."

"I'll manage that table," Aunt Sarah said. "But this furniture looks like it needs a little manpower. How about I call my boyfriend and his son to do the heavy lifting?"

Aaliyah and Nicole glanced at one another before turning back to Aunt Sarah. "You have a boyfriend?" Aaliyah asked. "Since when?"

"Since three months ago."

"Three months ago? Is that why you moved to LA?"

Aunt Sarah sheepishly looked at Aaliyah. "Maybe."

"Maybe?" Aaliyah walked over to her aunt. "When you told Dad and I that you needed this change and had to move to LA to fulfill a dream you had, you failed to mention anything about a boyfriend."

"That's because you would have thought I was crazy," Aunt Sarah said. "Sweetie, we can talk more about this later. For now, we have work to do."

Nicole placed a calming hand on Aaliyah's shoulder. Aaliyah's aunt meant everything to her, so she'd been devastated when her aunt informed the family that she wanted to move to LA. Especially since her aunt had given them a scare when she'd gotten extremely ill.

"Don't forget," Nicole whispered to Aaliyah, "Aunt Sarah has had a rough ten years. I know this is all a shock to you, but she needs some happiness in her life. Happiness that I'm sure she gets from having a companion."

The tension in her friend's shoulders lessened. "You're right," she said. Aaliyah walked over to Aunt Sarah. "I overreacted. We'd be happy to have your boyfriend and his son help us."

"Great." Aunt Sarah clasped her hands together. "Because they are right outside the door."

"Aunt Sarah," Aaliyah said as she placed her hands on her hips, "had you always planned to introduce us to your boyfriend today?"

Aunt Sarah shrugged. "Maybe, maybe not. Regardless, they are in the boutique now, so let's go."

As Nicole approached the boutique behind Aaliyah and Aunt Sarah, she was surprised that she knew one of the men talking to Kyra.

"I know you," Nicole said to the younger of the two gentlemen. "Isn't your name Bryant?"

The man squinted his eyes. "Do I know you?"

"We met at the bar a couple weekends ago, and I work with your cousin Kendrick."

"Ah, I see," he said. "So, we don't know each other. We just saw each other."

Wait, what? "Why does it always feel like you're offending me every time we talk?" she asked.

"Maybe the real issue is that you're too sensitive."

Nicole placed her hands on her hips. "Why are you always so rude?"

"Ignore my son," the older gentleman said as he extended his hand. "My name is Benjamin. You must be Nicole. It's nice to meet you."

"It's nice to meet you too."

"The world is so small," Kyra said. "I never met Benjamin and Bryant, but before you guys got here I was telling them about the Burrstones that I knew in Chicago and realized they were a part of that family."

"Really?" Aunt Sarah asked Benjamin.

"Yes, it's true. My sister and I were the only two of the Burrstone clan to move to California. Now, our children are here too."

"Yes, we are," Kendrick said as he approached from restroom area. Although she'd seen him at work earlier that day, it still caught her off guard when he approached.

Like at the bowling alley, the tattoos on his arms were exposed and the sight of the sexy ink made her mouth grow dry. She was a sucker for a guy with sexy tattoos, a goatee, broad shoulders, hypnotizing eyes and a body that she was sure could work hers in ways she never imagined.

Kendrick Burrstone was like a fantasy. A fantasy that she wanted to have every night with no interruptions.

"You okay?" he asked.

"Uh, yeah," she said, tuning back into the conversation that had continued without her.

"Does that plan work for everyone?" Aunt Sarah asked. Nicole nodded in agreement, although she had no idea what she was agreeing to.

"Great! Let's get to work."

Aaliyah pulled Nicole aside. "In case you weren't paying attention, Aunt Sarah suggested we break up into teams to get everything set up before the party starts in a couple hours. You and I are going to get our stations set up."

Nicole breathed a sigh of relief. "Thank goodness. I thought she was going to team me up with Kendrick, and there is only so much torture my lady parts can take from being that close to a man and not being allowed to touch him." Nicole had filled in Aaliyah and Kyra about Kendrick after she'd run into him her first day on set.

"Girl, nah," Aaliyah said. "I'm a free spirit full of energy, and Bryant is so serious and monotone. One conversation with the guy and he was drying up all of my happy energy. My aunt knew better than to team me up with him."

A voice directly behind them made them gasp in surprise.

"You shouldn't talk about people behind their backs," Bryant said, his eyes solely on Aaliyah.

"Yeah, well, you shouldn't sneak up on people. Were you trying to give us heart attack?"

"That wasn't my intention," he said, stepping closer to Aaliyah. "Forgive me?"

This dude is so intense. A part of Nicole was surprised that he'd apologized. She expected Aaliyah to respond right away, but instead, they both just seemed to be staring at each other. After almost a minute, Nicole felt more awkward than they looked. She jabbed Aaliyah in the side.

"Apology accepted," Aaliyah said. After Bryant had walked away, she whispered to Nicole. "What is it with the younger men in this family? They are attractive as hell, but it's obvious they don't know how to charm a woman."

Nicole didn't say anything. What could she say? Kendrick may have relationship issues, but he'd been slowly pulling her into his web of seduction ever since she'd spilled her drink all over his shirt.

"Are you sure you can't come to dinner with us?" Uncle Benjamin asked. After a successful launch party for the Bare Sophistication boudoir studio, he insisted on treating everyone to dinner.

"Sorry, Unc, I have to take a rain check. We start filming at 6:00 a.m. tomorrow, and I still have some prep work to do."

That was only partially true. All night, Kendrick's eyes had been glued to whatever Nicole was doing, whether it was talking to bloggers about the launch, customers eagerly signing up for appointments, or other local store owners who came by to show their support. Watching Nicole in action had been mesmerizing, so much so that Kendrick had to face a hard, true fact… His attraction to Nicole was not going to wear off anytime soon, so he better get used to the constant hard-on he had whenever she was in his vicinity.

"Okay, then, I'll catch you later," Uncle Benjamin said. Kendrick was almost out the door when his uncle called to him. "And walk Nicole home. She isn't going to dinner either."

"That's okay," Nicole said, swinging her purse over her shoulder. "I can walk myself. I'm only a few blocks away."

"Nonsense," Aunt Sarah said. "Kendrick will walk you, right, Kendrick?"

Shit. "Of course. Come on, LeBlanc. I'll keep you safe."

"Ha-ha," she said sarcastically. "Very funny."

Once they were outside, Kendrick welcomed the nice evening breeze. It was only ten at night, so the streets were littered with people either getting a late dinner or getting ready to party.

"To be so young again," Nicole said. He followed her line of vision to a group of guys and girls who looked no older than twenty-two.

"They're barely legal," Kendrick said. "I'd take thirty-five over those days, anytime."

"As far as my maturity level, I would too," Nicole said. "But I wouldn't mind having my twenty-one-year-old body again. You know what, scratch that. I miss my twenty-six-year-old body the most."

"I'm not sure what you miss about it," Kendrick said. "Your thirty-three-year-old body is putting those young bucks over there to shame."

When she smiled, Kendrick felt it all over his body.

"Thanks," she said. "Actually, the day I turned thirty, I knew that it was going to be a lot better than my twenties."

"How so?" he asked.

She glanced out at the street before looking at the sidewalk ahead of her. "I guess you could say that I was carrying a lot of baggage back then as a result of bad relationships, strained family relationships and friends who weren't necessarily good for me."

"I can relate on all accounts," Kendrick said as they turned a corner. "Except, my baggage carried on into my thirties too. It's only been a couple years that I've felt like I'm finally headed in the right direction."

"It's funny, isn't it?"

"What do you mean?" he asked.

Nicole brushed a few curls out of her face. "When you're in your twenties, everyone expects you to try and figure your life out so that you can be prepared for your future. Don't get me wrong, I know a lot of people who had everything figured out during that stage of their life. But, there are others who take longer to realize their potential, and I was one of those people. There were some days where I wanted to yell to the world, 'My name is Nicole and some things in my life are fucked up, but I'm working on it.'"

"I was one of those people too," Kendrick said. "Only in my case, I had a mother who was riding my ass about staying in school and making something of myself. You've already met my uncle and I'm sure you can tell that he's an amazing man, but he's not just that. He's a provider. He owns Burrstone Winery and Distillery and he built his business from the ground up. My mother—Uncle Benjamin's sister—is the same way. Right now, she's currently building a school in a small African village through the educational foundation that she started working with eighteen years ago."

"Your family sounds amazing."

"They are," he said. "They really are. And so are the rest who live in Chicago. We have family spread across the nation, doing good and living up to their potential."

"And you feel like you fall short," Nicole said. "Don't you?"

Kendrick took a deep breath. He never talked about this, but for some reason Nicole made him want to speak about it. "Yeah, I do. Unlike my cousins, I was the one who was constantly getting into trouble. My single mom raised me, and although she had the support of her family, she wanted to do everything on her own. I'm close to the Burrstone clan, but they are a no-nonsense bunch, and back in the day, I was getting into trouble left and right."

"I experienced something similar," Nicole said. "I'm close in age with one of my cousins who has always had everything together. When we were younger, I despised him because I didn't understand how he always seemed so sure of himself. He stayed with my grandparents for a couple years after my aunt had passed. Here I was searching for answers in all the wrong places, when he was going through life so confident. So focused. Despite the loss he'd suffered. I almost think that back then, having certain people in my life who understood my potential had a more negative impact on me than having people who didn't care if I achieved greatness or not."

"Growing up on the South Side of Chicago wasn't easy for me. I didn't understand why my cousins had a different life than I did. I didn't understand why my life didn't mirror the kind of happiness I saw reflected in their eyes whenever we went to barbecues. I became bitter of the circumstances I had to face and deal with that those around me didn't. After every family gathering in my grandparents' big suburban house, the streets were like a welcome-home gift. A heaven-sent one because the folks in the hood got me. They understood me. No one questioned why I wanted to cover my body in ink because they knew that each tattoo meant something personal to me. They knew that I wasn't purposely trying to fail my classes in school, but that the city didn't care about my school getting any funding, so my education wasn't important.

"I was a product of my environment, torn between what I knew and what I'd learned in the streets versus what my mom's family was trying to instill in me. It's difficult when you feel like you never fit in. What do you do when every facet in your life is pointing you in a different direction?"

"You wild out," Nicole said, nodding in understanding.

"Exactly. You try and fill that void however you can, counting the moments in which you actually feel fulfilled."

"Then when you do," she said, "you hold on to that moment with all you've got. I was probably holding on to more moments than I should have, until I finally learned a valuable lesson that I will never, ever forget."

"What did you learn?"

Nicole looked him in the eyes, the realness reflected in her gaze so strong it caught him off guard. "I realized that everyone who may rock with you is not always *for* you. There are people who will be placed in your life to teach you a lesson. Some will offer friendship. Others will be in the form of an enemy. Some may smile in your face, but talk about you behind your back. Others may even talk about you to your face. Only a select few are trying to help you. Encourage you. Uplift you. And within that group of individuals who are placed in your life for a reason—for a lesson—it's up to you to figure out what you can gain from each individual or situation to mold yourself into a better person and *not* the person they are trying to make you out to be."

Kendrick glanced at her, completely in awe at how raw and honest she was with her thoughts. They may have only been a couple years apart in age, but in that moment, he felt like she was years ahead of him in what she'd learned. He had no doubt that they'd both suffered a great deal of pain. Some self-inflicted, and pain brought on by others. He hoped one day he'd be able to peel back even more layers of Ms. Nicole LeBlanc.

"We crossed paths at the bar for a reason," he said to her when they neared what he assumed was her apartment complex.

"I know," she said with a smile. "We are meant to

help one another in some capacity. We just have to figure out what capacity that is."

His eyes dropped to her red-colored lips on their own accord. Per usual, they looked appetizing and *very* suckable.

"You're not going to ask me what flavor I'm wearing?"

Kendrick blinked a couple times. "Uh, flavored what?"

She giggled. "Your mind is in the gutter. I was talking about my lipstick. It's cherry in case you were wondering."

"I love cherry-flavored anything," he said, his eyes dropping to her lips again.

"Good to know."

They both grew silent again, each staring at the other with a newfound curiosity that Kendrick hoped they'd explore one day. *Kendrick, don't forget that you work together.* He'd had good reason for not dating— or kissing—coworkers, but at the moment he couldn't care less what that reason was.

Kendrick took a step closer to her, his nostrils filling with the sweet scent of her perfume.

"You smell divine," he said, his voice lower than he'd expected.

"You do too." She placed her hand on his arm, tracing the bottom of a tattoo that was peeking out from underneath his sleeveless shirt. Even though it was just his arm, her fingers left a heated path every place they touched.

"I'd love to see the entire tattoo one day," she said.

He smirked. "Maybe I'll show you sometime." *Right now, I have other things on my mind. Like how much does your lipstick taste like actual cherries.* Her breathing faltered the longer he stared at her lips.

He took another step closer and her chest grazed his. Even through her shirt, he could feel her nipples harden. "Remember when you just said we need to figure out why our paths crossed?" he asked.

"Yeah," she said breathlessly.

"I think I know where to start." Slowly, he dropped his head to hers. At the first touch of her lips to his, he knew he should have mentally prepared himself better for the kiss. He once heard someone say on one of those relationship reality shows that sparks were a real thing. Feeling fireworks when you kissed someone was a real thing. Forgetting about everything around you when your lips touched theirs was a real thing. Up until now, he would have called that person a liar.

He would have sworn up and down that there was no way that a kiss could completely knock you on your ass, but as he slipped his tongue in Nicole's mouth, that's precisely what happened. He was falling for her so hard, he didn't know how to catch himself. They still had more to learn about one another. He hoped his kiss didn't just reflect the fact that he liked the woman she was now, because that wasn't the case. What had him mesmerized and completely enthralled with her was the fact that she didn't let her past define her. She defined it. She'd taken the time to reflect on every stage in her life so that she could better prepare for the woman she wanted to be.

They said people couldn't reinvent themselves, but Nicole appeared to be doing just that. Or at least she was in the process of trying to do that. As he continued to kiss her with all the built-up sexual tension he felt, he realized that he needed to do some reevaluating on his own. Starting with his no dating coworkers rule.

Chapter 7

"Thanks so much, Nicole."

"You're welcome," Nicole said to Britt, one of the writers. "Enjoy your date."

I'd love to go on a date, she thought after Britt had left. It had been two days since Kendrick had kissed her outside her apartment, and it's all she'd been able to think about since it happened.

The studio was buzzing with excitement upon receiving news that the crew would head to Lake Tahoe this weekend to shoot the next commercial after the annual Gilbert Monroe Gala. Even better, they were allowed to bring a guest to the gala tomorrow night, so Nicole had decided to bring Kyra. They'd both been working long hours, so a night off would be nice.

Maybe I'll get some alone time with Kendrick. Lake

Tahoe was supposedly one of the most romantic places to visit, and even though they would be working, they'd have some free time too.

"Don't get ahead of yourself Nicole," she said aloud to herself. In the past, she'd been known to fall for a guy too fast and not based off the right reasons, despite her best intentions. Her friends would argue that it was her kryptonite. Meeting a guy and falling in love at the first sign of him giving her the attention she craved.

Nicole smiled when she thought about her friends Aaliyah, Danni and Summer. *I don't know what I'd do without those women.* Nicole never had any shortage of friends, but as she'd told Kendrick, everyone who rocked with her wasn't necessarily good for her. When she'd decided to take a step back from certain people in her life, unfortunately, that included some of the friends she'd grown up with. Men and women who never understood her desire to want more. To do more. To become more.

When you're stuck in a so-called rut called life, *it's hard to see past the blinds to look at what's beyond the window.* She'd known Danni back in high school, but they'd grown apart. Reconnecting with her had been one of the most rewarding relationships she'd gained in the past few years.

However, Aaliyah had come along and found a place in Nicole's heart. Not only was she a talented photographer, but she was a free spirit who never let anything stress her out. She now had people in her life that saw her purpose and although ending certain friendships was difficult, it was what she needed to do to see the light at the end of the tunnel.

"Am I interrupting?"

Nicole turned to face the beautiful older woman at the door. "No, not at all. How may I help you?"

The woman walked in wearing a bright yellow sundress with matching accessories. Her gorgeous gray curly hair was similar to the way Nicole liked to wear hers, and her warm smile was just as bright as her outfit.

"You must be Ms. Nicole," the woman said. "I've heard so much about you."

"You have. From who?" Nicole asked. She hadn't seen the woman at the studio before, and although she did look vaguely familiar, she couldn't place where she could've possibly met her before.

"Sorry, where are my manners." The woman reached out her hand. "I'm Felicia Burrstone, and I was just having lunch with my brother Ben and his girlfriend, Sarah. They raved about you, and rumor has it my son has taken a keen interest in you."

Kendrick's mom! Oh, crap! There was one thing that Nicole had never exceled at and that was meeting parents. She tended to do this awkward back and forth shuffle with her feet, and just when she would begin to feel comfortable, she'd mess it up by saying something inappropriate or offensive.

"Hello, Ms. Burrstone." Nicole shook her outstretched hand. "It's very nice to meet you. I've heard a lot about you. All good things. Your brother is so nice and I love Aunt Sarah. Well, she's not my aunt. She's my friend's aunt. But I treat her like she's my aunt—"

"Chile, breathe," Felicia said as she waved a hand in front of Nicole. "You'll pop a vein in your neck if you talk any faster."

"Sorry," Nicole said with a laugh. "I was just caught off guard. I didn't expect to meet you."

Felicia gave her a quick once-over. "I didn't expect my stubborn son to start dating someone while I was in Africa, so I guess we're both surprised. You're beautiful though. And talented, based off what I saw from the woman who just left here."

"Thank you," Nicole said. "You're beautiful, as well."

"Mom, what are you doing here?" Both women turned to face Kendrick in the doorway.

"Now is that any way to greet your mother?"

"Sorry," he said, walking in and giving her a hug. "Okay, now can I ask? What are you doing here?"

Felicia sat down in Nicole's styling chair. "Well, I came here to meet my son's girlfriend, whom everyone can't stop talking about since I landed early this morning."

"I'm not his girlfriend," Nicole said with more disappointment than she'd intended.

"But you want to be," Felicia said. "It's in your eyes."

"Mom, stop embarrassing her," Kendrick said.

"Oh, hush, son." Felicia pointed a finger at him. "Don't think I can't tell that you want to be her boyfriend just as badly. So, I don't know what you're waiting on. I'm ready for grandbabies and Nicole has nice child-bearing hips."

Kendrick did a face palm, causing Nicole to laugh. She'd never had this type of camaraderie with her own mother, so she found Felicia very charismatic.

"I was hoping the three of us could go out for dinner. The producer told me you're finished for the day."

"You talked to the producer?" Kendrick asked. "Why didn't you just ask me?"

"Because I didn't trust you not to lie. So, come on, you two, let's feed Mama and tell me all about how the two of you met."

Once Felicia was in the hallway, Kendrick pulled Nicole aside. "Are you okay with going to dinner with us?"

She took a deep breath, partially to compose her nerves having just met Kendrick's mom and partially because she wanted to breathe in Kendrick's seductive scent. "We actually have extra help in the boutique tonight, so I can go to dinner if you want me to." *Please say you do.*

"I would love it if you joined us," he said without hesitation.

It was on the tip of her tongue to ask him to repeat it just so she could be sure. She opened her mouth, but licked her lips instead. His eyes followed the movement of her tongue and before she could process what was happening, he pulled her in for a kiss that made her toes curl.

Just like their first kiss, she felt it in every fiber of her being. She came up on tiptoes and placed her hand behind his neck at the same time his hands went to her butt cheeks and pulled her closer. The move deepened their kiss even more.

"Mmm-hmm." Nicole and Kendrick broke apart at the sound of Felicia's voice. "Son, if you're going to stick your tongue that far down her throat, then you might as well just propose, get married and have babies already."

"Ma, give it up."

"Uh-oh," Felicia said, looking at Nicole. "When he calls me 'Ma,' he means business. Come on, y'all, I'm hungry."

"We're ready," Nicole said as she moved around Kendrick and joined his mom in the hallway.

"If you both smile any harder, I'm going to have to wear sunglasses."

"Ma."

"Okay, okay," Felicia said. "I'll save the rest of my jokes for the wedding."

"Your mom is a trip," Nicole said with a laugh as she leaned into Kendrick. "I love it."

Kendrick smiled. "Yeah, she's pretty awesome."

"And don't you two forget it," Felicia yelled, eliciting another laugh from them.

I could get used to this, Nicole thought.

"This is amazing," Kyra said when they walked into the gala at one of the largest hotels in downtown LA. Nicole had to admit that she was pretty blown away herself.

"Is your boyfriend here yet?"

Nicole rolled her eyes. "Why does everyone keep saying that? I don't want Kendrick thinking that I'm the one going around claiming he's my boyfriend."

"Okay, then," Kyra said. "Is the man who you like, would love to date and probably have dreams about sleeping with here yet?"

Nicole gave Kyra a blank stare. "Real cute."

"I try," she said with a smile. "But I answered my own question because I already see your boy toy over there."

Nicole followed the direction of Kyra's head nod. When she spotted Kendrick, her breath caught in her throat. "Oh, my, he looks so sexy." He was wearing a deep blue suit, and even from afar, she could tell that he'd gotten a haircut.

"I have to agree," Kyra said as she crossed her arms. "As nice as it was to see the tattoos on those masculine arms when he came to Bare Sophistication last week, it's mighty nice to see him rocking a suit. Tell me, why haven't y'all had sex yet?"

"We've barely acknowledged that we actually like each other," Nicole said.

"Which could be a good thing on your part."

Nicole glanced at Kyra. "What do you mean?"

"I know we haven't known each other long, but I met you when you were dating that knucklehead who cared more about his motorcycle collection than you. I'd only spent a week in Miami, but do you remember what you did that week?"

Nicole thought back to the time. "No, what did I do?"

"You enrolled in motorcycle lessons. The next time

we talked, you'd purchased a motorcycle and gotten your motorcycle license."

"So," Nicole said with a shrug. "I happen to love my motorcycle."

"Okay, then, what about the guy you dated before him? The fitness instructor you were obsessed with who was addicted to eating two raw eggs after every run. You aren't dating him anymore, and you still eat two raw eggs after every run."

"That's because it's good for you."

Kyra squinted. "Danni mentioned to Aaliyah and me one day that back in high school, you always hated raw eggs. In fact, you hated eggs period."

Hmm… I forgot I used to hate eggs. "My ex just opened my eyes to something I thought I didn't like. Now I like eggs."

Kyra glanced at the necklace Nicole was wearing. "What about your love for crystals?"

"I get it. Let's not go there," Nicole said with a strained laugh. "Even though you have a point, all of those things are a part of me now. My motorcycle. My love for eggs. My adoration for crystals and stones."

"I understand that," Kyra said, lightly gripping Nicole's hand. "And we all love you for the person you are and the obstacles you've had to overcome. I can tell Kendrick likes you and I know you like him. He may still have a few hang-ups about dating coworkers, and there's still a lot you don't know about him. I just want you to know that I—as well as others—can tell that Kendrick likes you for you. Don't feel as though you have to change yourself to please him or get his attention."

Nicole released a bit of the tension that had arisen during the start of their conversation. "I know, and I appreciate the reminder." She straightened her sleek gold-and-black dress and stood a little taller. "As much as I've grown, there's always more growing to do, but in this case, I'm just tired of all the sexual tension between us. I already know he wants me, but he needs a reminder that I won't wait around for him to make another move." Nicole looked his way and caught his eye. "I think that move should start with a dance."

"That's my girl," Kyra said with a smile. "While you're dancing with lover boy, I'll be making my rounds and networking."

"Sounds good."

"Oh, and another thing," Kyra said. "Try not to do that nervous laugh thing you do when a man starts flirting with you."

"Girl, please. I don't even do that anymore. We've been flirting for a couple weeks without any nervous laughter from me."

"Okay, just making sure. Go get him, girl."

Nicole walked in Kendrick's direction with a new-found goal to stop skidding around their attraction. Blame it on the fact that Valentine's Day was only a few weeks away. Blame it on the fact that three years ago, she'd made a promise to always go after what she wanted. Blame it on the fact that his kisses were so passionate that they rendered her speechless.

She could blame it on a list of things, but the truth

was plain and simple… *I want him. Badly.* If she had to sum up what she liked about Kendrick the most, it had to be his uncanny ability to understand her in ways others had failed to. She had more in common with him than she had with any man she'd ever met before. And surprisingly, she'd been herself since the day they met.

"Hey, guys," she said, walking up on Kendrick, Monty and Angelica.

"Hey, Nicole." Angelica gave her a quick hug. "You look gorgeous."

"Yes, she does," Kendrick said, looking her up and down before meeting her eyes. She was slightly taken aback by the fact that he wasn't hiding his attraction to her in front of his friends. "Are you having fun?"

"I just got here, but, yes, I am," she said with a laugh. As Kendrick continued to undress her with his eyes, she laughed again. Then again. And again. *Oh, crap! LeBlanc, get your shit together.*

"Are you okay?" he asked when her laugh turned into a giggle that was equally annoying when there was nothing to laugh at. *Oh, my God, seriously? I haven't had an unexplainable bout of laughter at all since I met Kendrick. This is soooo Kyra's fault for putting the idea in my head.*

"You look beautiful," Nicole said to Angelica, diverting the attention from herself and her awkward laugh. "Don't you agree, Monty? Isn't Angelica breathtaking tonight?"

All eyes turned to Monty, who'd already been staring a hole through Angelica. "Although she looks beautiful tonight," he said, "she's always breathtaking." Angelica gasped at the same time Nicole smiled. *Go, Monty!*

"Would you like to dance?" Monty asked.

"Um." Angelica quickly glanced at Nicole nervously. "Yes, I'd love to," she finally answered. Nicole and Kendrick watched Monty whisk Angelica away to the dance floor.

"Monty has waited years to tell Angelica how he feels," Kendrick said. "Maybe after tonight, he can finally be honest with her."

Nicole turned toward Kendrick. "Sometimes it's hard to be honest about your feelings, so I think the key is to not overthink it."

Kendrick's arm brushed against hers. "I know the feeling," he said. His voice deep. Sexy as hell. To her misfortune, she laughed again. And again.

"Are you laughing at me?" he asked. Instead of responding, she nodded to indicate that she was. Kendrick leaned down to her ear. "Keep laughing, and I'll do something to wipe the smile off your face."

Nicole gasped. *And cue more awkwardness.* She slipped her hand into Kendrick's. "Let's dance." Luckily, he let her drag him to the dance floor. The moment they were on the dance floor, the song changed to one that was an even slower than the one before.

"May I?" Kendrick asked, extending his arms.

Don't laugh. Just respond normally. "Yes, you may." *You go, girl! Mission accomplished!*

His hands fit perfectly around her waist just as hers did around his neck. She leaned her head against his chest as they began to sway to the song.

"I've missed you," he said.

She smiled. "You just saw me last night."

"I had to share you with my mom," he said. "And everyone knows Felicia leads the conversation whenever she's in the room."

"I enjoyed talking to your mom. She reminds me a lot of my grandmother."

"Does your grandmother still live in Miami?"

"She sure does." Nicole thought about her grandmother. "My grandfather passed away about ten years ago, and it took my gran a while to get over his passing. Now, she's dating a guy she met in one of her cooking classes."

"Why do I get the feeling that you're a lot like your gran?"

"I am and she's my world…" Her voice trailed off as she thought of her mom. *Please don't ask me about my mom*, she thought. *Not tonight.*

"You feel so good," Kendrick said, bringing her closer to him. "I'm not sure dancing with you in public was such a good idea."

Nicole lifted her head to meet his gaze. "Why is that?"

He studied her eyes. "I'd say that to the outside eye, it probably looks like we're completely engrossed in one another right now."

She slowly exhaled. "For you, is that far from the truth?" He was so close, his minty breath tickled her lips.

"Quite the opposite, LeBlanc," he said in a rugged voice. "Not only am I completely engrossed in you, but I'm beyond intrigued and fascinated to peel back more of your layers."

She swallowed the lump in her throat. "You've had my permission to peel back those layers since the day we met."

He lifted an eyebrow. "Why do I get the feeling we're talking about more than getting to know one another on a psychological level?"

Nicole pulled his ear closer to her mouth. "That's because we've done a lot of talking. Reaching a psychological euphoria wasn't exactly on my mind tonight."

Kendrick groaned. "You shouldn't have said that."

She shivered. *Don't laugh. Don't laugh.* A couple seconds later, she laughed.

Kendrick squinted his eyes. "Why do you keep laughing at me?"

Because you make me nervous, and when I'm nervous, I laugh. And once the crazy laughter starts, it's hard to cut off. Instead of explaining that, she laughed again.

"I have an idea," he said as he led her out a side door of the ballroom. He walked with urgency, yet, he kept a normal pace. The sexual tension crackling around them was at an all-time high, neither speaking as Kendrick opened door after door of meeting rooms that were around the corner from the ballroom.

The last door on the left was supposedly what he was looking for. He pulled her through the door, shutting it behind them. Nicole backed into the wall, curious to see where this was going.

"Why are we here?" she asked.

"I think you know." He studied her eyes. "I wanted to get you all to myself without any interruptions."

"Oh." Nicole shuffled from one heel to the other, reminding herself to breathe. However, the longer he watched her. Observed her. The more nervous energy she had. On cue, she laughed again.

"What did I tell you about laughing at me?"

"I can't help it," Nicole said. "When I find something funny, I laugh about it."

"So you find me funny?"

"In a way, yes, I do," she said.

"Well, let me refresh your memory about what I said earlier." Kendrick leaned closer, placing his arms on either side of her. "Before we started dancing, I warned you that the next time you laughed at me, I would do something to wipe the smile from your face."

Nicole took a deep breath. "I think you're all talk, and I'm tired of talking."

He raised an eyebrow. "You're tired of talking?"

"Sure am," she said with more confidence than she felt. "And if you're trying to make me nervous, it's not going to work."

His lips curled to the side in a sexy smirk, and his eyes darkened even more. "Nicole, when you look back at this moment, I want you to remember how you feel right now. Remember how my arms felt holding you hostage in your place." His mouth got closer to her neck, but he didn't kiss her. "Remember how my breath felt as it tickled the dark-brown curls resting on your neck."

By now, she was reminding herself *how* to breathe,

but she was doing a terrible job. Her goal had been to take the flirting they had been doing since they met to another level. Yeah, maybe she had been trying to break his control, but who wouldn't with a guy who looked as sexy as Kendrick?

His mouth paused right in front of hers. "But mainly, I want you to remember that I gave you fair warning that if you pushed me to this point, I was damn sure gonna to push back."

Nicole gasped, unable to speak. She didn't see the next move coming until her feet were off the ground.

Chapter 8

Kendrick dragged his lips to hers while he lifted her off the ground. An empty meeting room in a crowded hotel wasn't exactly ideal for what he had in mind, but he was past the point of waiting.

When he reached the table in the middle of the room, he gently placed her on top of it, mentally thanking the designers of the room for putting dim lights along the walls. It wasn't that he needed illumination for what he planned on doing, but he didn't want to miss a moment, and his eyes hadn't adjusted in the darkness yet.

He ran his hands up and down her thick thighs while her hands gripped his neck even harder. *Damn, she kisses with so much passion.* It was something he'd already experienced from her, but it caught him off guard nonetheless. If he kept on kissing her, he'd get too lost to continue with his plan.

His lips left hers and continued down her collarbone, marking a path to her plump breasts and that tattoo he liked so much.

"It's a scorpion," he stated right before he placed a kiss on it.

"It is," she said breathlessly. "I'm a Scorpio."

"That explains so much," he said before bringing his lips back to hers. After a few more seconds, he lifted his head so that he could look her in the eyes. "Are you game to see what I want to do next?" If she had any objections, he would stop right now.

He watched her eyes darken in the dim lighting. "I'm game," she said, pulling him in for another kiss. Their tongues intertwined, each stroke eliciting more passion and promise.

Once again, Kendrick left her lips, leaving a trail of kisses on her collarbone and breasts. Slowly, he eased the fabric of her dress up her thighs until it was scrunched around her waist. He kissed the insides of her thighs in a way that had Nicole panting on the table.

"I got you," he said when she shivered as he got closer to his point of interest. When his hands found her panties, he began sliding them down her legs. "Want me to stop?" he asked.

"Hell, no," she said in a clear voice. "Don't stop."

When her panties were removed, he ran his fingers up and down her core, stopping at the part he knew would drive her crazy with need. Lowering his head, he smiled at the way her knees each fell to the side in anticipation.

I could stay like this forever, he thought as he positioned himself in between both thighs. "I've been dying to know how you taste." He flicked his tongue over her nub. Nicole bucked off the table just as he hoped she would.

Kendrick placed his hands under both her butt cheeks and suckled the sensitive nub before licking her with long languid strokes. In the back of his mind he still remembered his golden rule about not dating anyone he worked with, but he could no longer restrain himself when he was around Nicole.

And it wasn't just because she was drop-dead gorgeous with her creamy brown skin, soft beautiful curls, sexy tats and lips he couldn't stop kissing. A huge reason why it was so hard for him to stay away was that he couldn't deny how well they meshed together. They exuded the same vibes. Talking to one another was easy and not forced at all. With Nicole, he felt like he could be himself, and they had more in common than he'd had with anyone he'd dated in the past.

You should be dating her. Despite how much he liked Nicole, they currently weren't committed to each other. He hadn't even flirted with another woman since he'd met Nicole, much less go out. However, imagining her dating anyone was a thought he didn't even want to think about. Being around her was reminding him of what he'd been missing the past couple years.

Kendrick had never been the type to date multiple women, but after getting his heart broken one too many times, he'd begun to think that not committing was exactly what he should to be doing. The problem with not committing to one woman meant he would never find that rare connection or chemistry with anyone.

In a lot of ways, he used his black book as a shield to guard his heart. If he went into the situation with eyes wide open, then he wouldn't be blindsided. There was no one in his black book with whom he wanted to be in a relationship, and therefore he'd never gotten attached.

You're growing attached to the woman who is moaning and clenching your head right now. He'd liked Nicole so much when he met her, he never even put her number in his black book. She'd gotten inserted straight into his phone contacts. *You should have known then she was different, my dude.*

Nicole adjusted her legs in a way that let him know she was close. It took a few seconds for him to realize she was scooting away from his mouth. "What's wrong?" he asked.

Glazed over eyes met his. "It's been so long… It feels so good… I can't take it."

He smirked. "How long has it been?"

"Um, I don't know. One year. Maybe two. Maybe more. I didn't keep count."

Nicole was so intuitive and in touch with her body, he highly doubted she didn't remember, but he wouldn't give her a hard time about it.

"Let's fix that." Encircling her ankle with his hand, he pulled her back to his awaiting mouth, continuing his strokes quicker than before.

"Kendrick, oh, my… It's… I'm going to…"

He knew what she was trying to say, and he couldn't deny that it was music to his ears. Nicole bucked her hips against his mouth again, meeting him lick for lick. Without warning, he added two fingers to the mix as his mouth stayed fixated on her nub.

"Oh, shit." Expletives rang from her mouth like a sexy song of passion, mixing with her moans and serenading his ears in a way he knew would be branded in his mind for a long time. When she finally released her orgasm, Kendrick was glad that all the other meeting rooms along the hallway were empty. He had no doubt that someone would have heard had they been occupied.

Kendrick only lowered her back to the table when he'd made sure he didn't leave one last drop. He wasn't exactly sure what he expected Nicole to say or do next, but pulling down her dress, getting off the table and gently pushing his back to the wall was not what he thought would happen.

There weren't many times that Nicole would completely disregard her expensive dress and rough carpeted floor to get on her knees, but tonight was that night.

She didn't even have the words to express what Kendrick had just done to her. She was still shivering with after effects of her orgasm but being in a public place meant time was limited, so she needed to make the next move.

"You think they have cameras in here?" she asked as she began to slide down his body to the floor.

His eyes grew big. "I don't… I don't know. Do you want to leave?"

"Not a chance," she said as she began unbuttoning his pants. His shaft was straining against his boxers. Her mouth watered at the sight.

"You don't have to do this," he said. "Like I said, I was dying to taste you, but I didn't expect anything in return."

Nicole smiled. "What if I've been dying to taste you just as bad?" She lowered his boxers and took him in her hands, relishing in the size of him. *Oh, this is going to be good.* She quickly licked his tip in preparation. When she looked up at him, his eyes were glued to her movements, so she licked it again.

Kendrick threw his head back against the wall. "That shit was sexy as hell."

Nicole slowly lowered her mouth over him inch by inch, breathing in a way that expanded her throat to take him in as much as possible. Once she had him in as far as he would go, she began rolling her tongue up and down his shaft.

She heard noise on the other side of the door, but ignored it. After the mind-blowing orgasm she'd just experienced, she wanted Kendrick to feel just as good.

She fondled him in her hands in the same circular motion as her mouth and was rewarded with an animal-like groan from Kendrick.

"Your mouth feels amazing," he said in a deep voice. One of the things that Nicole was starting to like more and more about Kendrick was the different levels of his deep baritone voice. Sure, lots of women were fans of men with deep voices, but to her, Kendrick's took the cake.

The tone of his voice held purpose. Mystery. His voice was confident, yet vulnerable when needed. Strong, yet soft if he needed to whisper. Had he not chosen to work behind the scenes, Nicole was sure he could have been an actor with his good looks and swoon-worthy voice.

"Damn, Nicole."

Two words. He'd only said two words to her, yet those words caused her to increase the intensity and speed of her tongue and hand strokes. His leg jerked, proving he was getting closer to his release. She briefly glanced up at him to see the emotions that crossed his face and noticed that he'd lifted his shirt, displaying a striking set of abs.

Beautiful, she thought. Beautiful wasn't a term used on manly and rugged men such as Kendrick, but that's exactly what he looked like right now. Typically, when a man was about to climax, they did what Nicole coined The Ugly Betty. Their eyes started rolling in the back of their head, their mouth grew slack, they started panting and then finally all those things merged together in a convulsing mess that was *not* attractive.

Maybe it wasn't fair to say that Kendrick didn't display any signs of The Ugly Betty since they still hadn't had sex yet. However, right now, in this moment, his face was intense yet controlled, and to Nicole, he looked downright beautiful.

"Nicole, baby," Kendrick said. "You should probably stop now. I'm getting close."

Instead of heeding his warning, she increased her movements even more.

"Nicole."

Not listening.

"Nicole."

Still not listening.

"Shit. Nicole."

Once again, not listening, but you're too late anyway. Kendrick bucked off the wall, gripping the table for support. His eyes were wild and in disbelief that she hadn't released him as he'd warned.

"That was… Amazing," he said as he began to come down from his passionate high.

"Aren't you glad I didn't stop?" she teased.

"I'll get you back," he said, fixing his clothes. "Sooner than you think."

Nicole adjusted her dress back and made sure that her curls weren't in complete disarray. "Promises, promises."

Kendrick laughed. "Let's get out of her before anyone wonders where we've been."

"Sounds good," she said as she followed Kendrick. They both froze in their tracks the moment he opened the door.

"Uh, hi," one of the two hotel employees standing there said. "We, uh, we heard noise in the meeting room, but once we figured out what it was, we didn't want to interrupt. We only waited because we have to set up the room tonight for an early-morning meeting."

Nicole and Kendrick looked at each other, then back at the employees. "Um, we appreciate that." Although

Kendrick was the one who addressed them both, they were only looking at Nicole. On instinct, she smoothed out her already smooth dress and stepped a little closer to Kendrick.

"The room is yours," Kendrick said to the young male employees before motioning for Nicole to walk ahead of him and back to the ballroom. "Try not to drool too much, boys."

"You're my hero," one of them said.

"Adult goals," the other said.

When Nicole and Kendrick turned the corner, they both let out the laughs they'd been holding in.

"Oh, my God, that was so embarrassing," Nicole said. "How much do you think they heard?"

"Enough that they knew better than to interrupt." Kendrick gave her a quick kiss. "And you look so damn good they didn't know what to do with themselves. I was tempted to remind them to pick their jaws off the floor."

As they walked back to the ballroom, they were both still laughing. "I guess I can get through the rest of the party now," Nicole said.

"I'm not sure I can." Kendrick leaned toward her ear. "If we get bored within the next hour, I'll race you to the other end of the hotel to check for any more unlocked doors."

A sly smile crossed Nicole's face. "You're on."

Chapter 9

Nicole grabbed her purse and roller suitcase when her Uber driver pulled up in front of Bare Sophistication.

"Call me if you need anything," Nicole said after she gave Kyra a quick hug and waved goodbye to the other employees.

"I have everything covered, and I want you to have a good time. But don't worry, I'll call if I need anything."

At the mention of the word *fun*, she smiled. A couple nights ago, she'd had a lot of fun with Kendrick. Granted, she'd planned on acting on her attraction and not tiptoeing around it; however, she'd hadn't thought that Kendrick would have had seduction plans of his own.

Kyra walked closer to her so no one else could hear. "Based off that dreamy look on your face, I have a feeling you're going to have *a lot* of fun. When you get back, Aaliyah will be here and we expect the inside scoop."

"Y'all are too much." She handed her bag and suitcase to the Uber driver, told him what airline she was taking and got in the backseat.

Pulling out her small cosmetic bag and compact mirror, she began applying some lip and eye makeup. She probably spent more time putting on makeup in the car than she did at home. Makeup—whether she was applying it to herself or someone else—always made her feel better, and right about now, she needed a little makeup courage.

In all honesty, she was a little nervous about what Lake Tahoe would bring. She would be there to work on the commercial and part of the documentary they were shooting, yet all she could think about was if she and Kendrick would pick up where they left off at the gala or if they'd keep it strictly professional.

Whenever her mind was racing with thoughts and scenarios, there was only one person in her life whose soothing voice always seemed to calm her nerves. Reaching in her purse, she took out her iPhone and dialed her gran's number. Dorothy Meech answered on the second ring.

"There's my girl." Her gran's sweet voice poured from the phone. "How's my sweet pea doing in Hollywood?"

"I'm doing good, Gran. I'm actually headed to Lake Tahoe right now to shoot a commercial and part of the documentary."

"Oh, that sounds wonderful! Have you met any famous people yet?"

"I haven't met Denzel Washington if that's what you're asking, but I've met a few celebrities at industry events and seen them at restaurants." Gran had loved Denzel Washington for as long as Nicole could remember and owned all his movies.

"Shoot, I was hoping you would tell me you met Denzel and slipped him my number."

"Dorothy, I heard that," said a male voice in the distance.

Nicole laughed. "Tell your boyfriend, Mike, I said hi."

"He heard you, sweet pea. I have you on speakerphone."

"Hi, Mike," she said.

"Hi, Nicole. Glad to hear everything is going well in Hollywood. We miss you here in Miami."

"I miss you both too, but I hope you're keeping my gran out of trouble."

"I try my best," Mike said. "But you know how stubborn your gran can be."

"Trust me, I know." Nicole grew quiet before speaking again. "Listen, I don't want to interrupt, so I'll let you two go. Gran, I'll call or text you when I arrive in Lake Tahoe."

"Hold on, sweet pea," Gran said before asking Mike if they could have some privacy. "Okay, it's just you and I now. What's wrong? I can hear it in your voice."

Nicole smiled. Leave it to Gran to always pick up on it when something was bothering her. "There isn't really anything wrong, but I'm confused about something and I'm not sure what to do next."

"Go ahead," Gran encouraged. "Spit it out."

Nicole fidgeted with the strap of her purse. "So, there's this guy I met out here and I really like him."

"What's the problem? Does he not like you back?"

"No, he likes me back. The problem is that we both work together. But when we first met we didn't know we worked together. Once we found out, he became distant and was avoiding me, until…" her voice trailed off.

"Until he wasn't avoiding you anymore," Gran finished.

"Exactly. We've gotten closer over the past couple weeks, but we haven't really had a serious conversation about where we stand or if the working together thing is still an issue. I mean… I'm only working with the crew for the next week and a half."

"And that's a problem?"

"It is, but I also heard that it's possible that The Gilbert Monroe Agency may offer me a full-time position?"

"If that's the case, do you plan on staying in Hollywood for a while?"

"I don't know, Gran. All of this was supposed to be temporary, and they may not even ask me to join the agency permanently. Staying full-time changes everything. Most of my work is in Miami. My life is in Miami. My friends are in Miami."

"You're a freelance makeup artist and hairstylist, and although you have independently grown your brand and are making your mark in the industry, you can make your mark anywhere. How is the Bare Sophistication pop-up doing?"

"It's doing great! So is the boudoir studio portion since we only schedule those clients when Aaliyah is in town and I'm not working on set."

"I gathered as much when I spoke with Sarah," Gran said. Aunt Sarah and Gran had formed a friendship after her and Aaliyah had become friends a few years ago. "Listen, sweet pea, most of your life you've been afraid of change, and although I understand why, as your gran, it's my duty to make sure you go after your dreams. Don't lose sight of what's best for you because you're scared of failing."

"But what if that happens?" Nicole asked. "What if I do fail?"

"That's not possible. You're talented and creative. You were born to do this. You were born to succeed in whatever you put your mind to. And despite all your growth, you fail to realize one important fact about yourself."

Nicole blinked back an unshed tear. "And what is that?"

"Sweet pea, I love you with all my heart. But your biggest challenge hasn't been that you are afraid you'll fail. I've seen you fail before, and whether you admit it or not, you're comfortable with failing. It's almost as if you expect you'll fail sometimes." Nicole felt in her heart what Gran was going to say before she even said it.

"Your biggest challenge has always been your fear

of succeeding. Because if you succeed, that means you must face some hard truths about your character, and you can't hide behind being afraid. You've grown so much from the scared and angry teen who came to live with your grandfather and I all those years ago, and all I want for you, sweet pea, is for you to continue to shine. Everything will work out the way it should."

Nicole wiped the lone tear that had fallen on her cheek. "I love you, Gran."

"I love you too, sweet pea."

After Nicole ended the call, she let Gran's words sink in. Gran always knew exactly what to say to her to bring everything into perspective.

"We're here," the Uber driver said as he stepped out to help her with her suitcase.

"Thank you," she said.

"You're welcome." He started walking back to the driver's side, but stopped. "And for what it's worth, miss, I don't think you should worry about failing. Take it from someone who is just starting to realize at age fifty what he wishes he knew at twenty. Taking chances is scary, but worth the risk."

On one hand, she was slightly creeped out that he'd probably listened to her entire conversation; on the other hand, it was her fault because she was the one who had a private conversation in his car.

"Thanks for telling me that."

"You're welcome," he said. "Thanks for one of the more enlightening rides I'll have today. Enjoy your trip."

I'll try, she thought. Her nerves had calmed since

Dear Reader,

IT'S A FACT: if you answer 4 quick questions, we'll send you 4 **FREE REWARDS!**

I'm not kidding you. As a leading publisher of women's fiction, we value your opinions… and your time. That's why we are prepared to **reward** you handsomely for completing our mini-survey. In fact, we have 4 Free Rewards for you, including 2 free books and 2 free gifts.

As you may have guessed, that's why our mini-survey is called **"4 for 4".** Answer 4 questions and get 4 Free Rewards. It's that simple!

Thank you for participating in our survey,

Pam Powers

To get your 4 FREE REWARDS:
Complete the survey below and return the insert today to receive 2 FREE BOOKS and 2 FREE GIFTS guaranteed!

"4 for 4" MINI-SURVEY

1 Is reading one of your favorite hobbies?
☐ YES   ☐ NO

2 Do you prefer to read instead of watch TV?
☐ YES   ☐ NO

3 Do you read newspapers and magazines?
☐ YES   ☐ NO

4 Do you enjoy trying new book series with FREE BOOKS?
☐ YES   ☐ NO

YES! I have completed the above Mini-Survey. Please send me my 4 FREE REWARDS (worth over $20 retail). I understand that I am under no obligation to buy anything, as explained on the back of this card.

168/368 XDL GMYK

FIRST NAME	LAST NAME

ADDRESS

APT.#	CITY

STATE/PROV.	ZIP/POSTAL CODE

READER SERVICE—Here's how it works:

BUSINESS REPLY MAIL
FIRST-CLASS MAIL   PERMIT NO. 717   BUFFALO, NY

POSTAGE WILL BE PAID BY ADDRESSEE

READER SERVICE
PO BOX 1341
BUFFALO NY 14240-8571

NO POSTAGE
NECESSARY
IF MAILED
IN THE
UNITED STATES

her conversation with Gran, but she doubted they would go away completely anytime soon.

"Kendrick, is this how you envisioned them standing?"

He glanced at the bundled-up couple who were minutes away from having a scripted snowball fight that would be captured on camera.

"Switch the location of the man and woman," he said, just as Nick, the director, joined them on set.

One day, Kendrick thought as Nick took his seat. He liked Nick, and as a director and creative director duo, they worked well together and tended to have the same vision. However, Kendrick still hoped that after this series of Valentine's Day commercials and documentary, he'd land a head director role and then eventually producer role.

"And action," Nick said. They were at one of the most beautiful and romantic lodge resorts in Lake Tahoe shooting a commercial highlighting all the resort and area had to offer. They still had to shoot the second half of the commercial early tomorrow before they would be able to solely focus on the documentary.

After a few takes, makeup was requested for a touch-up. *Damn, she looks good.* As soon as everyone had arrived at the resort, it had been all hands on deck, so Kendrick hadn't gotten a chance to speak to Nicole yet.

He watched her walk on set in a pair of fashionable beige-and-brown boots with matching coat. Her curls were sticking out from under her hat, but what really had him squirming in his seat was the nude lipstick she was wearing. *I wonder what flavor it is?*

After she finished touching up the actor and actress, she left the set, passing by his creative director chair as she did. Her lips curled to the side in a smile as she mouthed the word *hi*.

What flavor? he mouthed back, hoping she understood him. Her eyes softened before she mouthed, *vanilla and hot chocolate.* He lifted his eyebrow in a way that he hoped let her know that he planned on finding out precisely how that combination tasted after they finished shooting for the day.

Hot chocolate indeed, he thought as she walked back to the warming trailer. It was forty degrees outside, which was much colder than Kendrick would have liked. Luckily, he'd grown up in Chicago so he was used to the cold weather unlike some of the crew who were caught off guard by the chill.

You need the cold air to cool you off anyway. Kendrick had always been able to control his emotions and desires. It was something he'd learned from his mom. Felicia Burrstone was a survivor, and she never let anyone see her vulnerabilities. He'd run across his fair share of beauties in the industry, and had always managed to downplay his interest and stick to his golden rule. *Except now...* Being around Nicole was a job in and of itself because his entire body awakened whenever she was in a room with him. It was like a switch he couldn't cut off because no matter how many times he flipped the switch down, the light remained on.

After four more hours, they'd finally finished filming the couple participating in a variety of outdoor activities. "That's all for today, folks," Nick said. "We'll resume bright and early tomorrow."

"Are you okay, man?" Monty asked, walking over to Kendrick.

"Of course. Why do you ask?"

Monty smiled. "Maybe because you seemed to be several miles away during the entire commercial today. Physically, you were here. But mentally, you were someplace else. Could it be that a pretty lady is occupying all your thoughts?"

Kendrick shrugged. "I don't know what you're talking about."

"Come on, lay off it," Monty said with a laugh. "You and Nicole disappeared for almost an hour at the gala, and all day today, you both were shooting each other those *come hither* looks."

"Come hither?" Kendrick shook his head. "I need you to lay off reading the romance novels because they are making you say things like *come hither*."

"There's nothing wrong with a man reading a little romance," Monty said, causing Kendrick to laugh louder than he'd intended.

Monty placed his hand on Kendrick's shoulder and turned him to where Nicole was standing and talking to Angelica. "All I'm saying is that those lovesick puppy eyes that you've been shooting her way since she walked into the studio was cute at first, but now, I'm just worried that you're taking too long to claim her." It was then that Kendrick noticed that Nick was also standing with the ladies, his eyes solely focused on Nicole.

"You're one to talk," Kendrick said. "Have you told Angelica how you feel yet?"

"Not yet, but I will."

Kendrick frowned. "Listen to you, telling me what to do when you haven't even taken your own advice." Just then Terrance, another cameraman, walked up to the ladies and said something to make Angelica laugh.

"Oh, hell, nah," Monty said, hitting Kendrick on the shoulder. "Come on. Let's go get our women and take them to dinner before Batman and Robin swoop in and whisk them away to the bat cave."

Kendrick shook his head. "Man, where do you come up with this stuff?"

Monty pointed to his head. "This brain is full of jokes, metaphors and useless information. But right now, the only thing on my mind is saving my girl from Robin."

"Then maybe you should tell her how you feel tonight. You two seemed real cozy at the gala."

Monty glanced from the women to Kendrick. "Tell you what. If you admit that you want to commit to dating Nicole, then I'll tell Angelica how I feel tonight."

"Okay," Kendrick said with a shrug. "I admit that I want to commit to dating Nicole."

"What?" Monty said. "Man, I thought you were going to hesitate or spit that stupid rule about not dating anyone you work with."

Kendrick looked at Nicole and caught her eye. "Nah,

man, I couldn't avoid that woman any more if I tried. I planned her telling her tonight."

Monty hesitantly glanced at Angelica. "Guess that means I need to man up."

Kendrick slapped a hand on the back of Monty's shoulder. "That's exactly what it means. Let's see if what you've been reading in any of those romance novels helps you open up to Angelica about your feelings."

"They better," Monty said as they walked over to the women.

"Hey, ladies," Kendrick said. "Monty and I were wondering if the two of you would do us the honor of accompanying us to dinner tonight."

Nick cleared his throat. "Terrance and I were just about to ask you ladies the same thing."

Nicole and Angelica looked from one set of men to the other before they looked at each other. "Sorry," Angelica said to Nick and Terrance. "We were planning on going to dinner with Kendrick and Monty."

"Oh," Terrance said. "But they only just asked you."

"Yup," Nicole replied. "And we've accepted their offer."

"We get the hint," Nick said before he and Terrance turned to leave the group.

"Well played," Nick said in a low voice that only Kendrick heard. He didn't say anything in response to Nick's comment. Saying *you might as well move on to someone else* seemed a bit much, considering he still had to have a serious conversation with Nicole.

"How about we all change and meet in the lobby in an hour?" Angelica suggested. They each nodded in agreement. Kendrick was looking forward to having dinner with Nicole and his friends, but he'd much rather have Nicole all to himself.

Chapter 10

"You told her that story?" Kendrick asked Monty. "What happened to the bro code?"

"I'm glad Monty told me," Nicole said as she took a sip of her wine. "It's probably one of the funniest stories I've ever heard."

During speed dating, Monty had told Nicole about the time when they had been shooting a commercial in a desert and the Porta Potti had broken. They had a bathroom in each of the trailers, but the line was long during our break and Kendrick couldn't wait.

"My mom had just gotten back from one of her overseas educational adventures, and she wanted me to do a cleanse with her. I'd juiced before, but I'd never done a cleanse, so how was I supposed to know what it would do to me?"

"It was the funniest thing," Angelica said with a laugh. "In the distance, there was a closed down gas station that the crew had passed on our way to the location where we were shooting that day. All I see is Kendrick hightailing it in the desert, running as fast as he could to the gas station."

"The bathroom was disgusting," he said. "But at least the lock had been broken and I was able to go in there."

"The last thing he expected to do was to accidently turn on his walkie-talkie," Monty said with a laugh. "We're all standing around, waiting to get back to shooting when we suddenly heard groans, moans and expletives coming from Kendrick's walkie-talkie."

Even though she'd already heard the story, she was laughing harder than she had the first time.

Kendrick shook his head. "It was the first project I'd worked on with most the crew, and I figured after that the teasing would be brutal."

"But he was never teased that much… At least not to his face," Angelica said.

"Why was that?" Nicole asked. "I would have assumed you would have been teased pretty badly."

"Look at him," Angelica said. "He was still one of the hottest guys to join the agency, and with all his tats and his edgy personality, it didn't take long for women to start giving him attention."

"Right," Monty said. "And I guess if you can broadcast your entire intimate bathroom talk to an entire crew and still get ladies' attention, other men thought better of teasing him."

Nicole glanced at Kendrick and met his gaze. Tonight he was wearing another sleeveless shirt with his tats peaking beneath the edges. He either just got better looking every time she saw him, or her feelings for him were growing quicker than she realized. "I can understand the attention," she said, maintaining eye contact as she took another sip of her wine.

"That dinner was amazing," Angelica said. "I heard they have an indoor rooftop garden across from the bar. I think it's open another hour. Should we check it out?"

"Yeah, let's," Nicole agreed. Monty and Kendrick settled the check, and the four of them headed to the elevators.

"You look beautiful," Monty said to Angelica after they boarded the elevator.

"Thanks," she said with a smile. "You look handsome, as well."

Nicole's reflection caught Kendrick's in the mirrored wall. Neither said anything, but then again, no words were really needed.

Once they arrived at the rooftop garden, Monty and Angelica walked one way, while Kendrick and Nicole walked another.

"You did good today," Nicole said. "Especially since you had to direct outside in the cold."

"You want to know what kept me warm?" Kendrick asked. "Seeing you in those sexy brown snow boots and knowing that you were purposely walking in a way that would keep my eyes glued to your ass."

Her laugh echoed in the garden. "I was not taunting you with my ass."

"Yes, you were," Kendrick said. "And apparently, I wasn't the only one to notice since Nick didn't waste any time approaching you after we wrapped up today."

Nicole smirked. "Do I sense a little jealousy, Kendrick Burrstone?"

"Maybe," he said with a shrug. "Whether it's true or not, you chose to go to dinner with me so I'm not concerned with Nick. But this brings up a good point."

"What's that?"

Kendrick pointed to a bench that was in the corner of the garden. Once they were both seated, he continued. "Do you remember what I said about not dating people I work with?"

Crap, does he want to end this before we even get started? "Yes, I remember."

"Well," he continued. "What would you say if I told you I was wrong?"

Nicole lifted an eyebrow. "Can you be a little more specific?"

"Of course." He leaned back on the bench and draped an arm across the back. "Nicole, I did create my rule for a reason, but I was wrong... You are amazing. Talented. Beautiful. You make me laugh... I'm pretty sure I make you laugh too, given that you can't stop laughing at me sometimes."

On cue, she laughed again.

"If you're interested," he said, "I would love for us to date and see where this goes."

Her heart beat faster. "Are you sure you're okay with taking things a step further?"

Kendrick laughed. "I kinda thought we already had."

Her cheeks grew warm as she thought about the gala. She scooted closer to Kendrick on the bench. "In that case, I'd have to say I'm on board with that suggestion."

His smile brightened his entire face. "I was hoping you would say that." When he leaned in for a kiss, she was already meeting him halfway.

It was another busy day in Lake Tahoe for the crew. All morning had been spent finishing the second part of the resort's commercial, and now they were all gathered at a quaint cabin about fifteen minutes from the resort to film a part of the documentary.

The Gilbert Monroe Agency had teamed up with a major television network for a documentary about the true meaning of love, which would be aired and streamed online on Valentine's Day.

All the couples featured in the documentary had submitted videos about their relationship and view on love and were chosen by a panel of judges that were comprised of Gilbert Monroe employees and employees of the television network.

Home owners of the quaint cabin, Mr. and Mrs. Saunders, served as a focal point for the documentary.

"Who wants some hot chocolate with marshmallows?" Mrs. Saunders asked the crew as she lugged in a tray of empty mugs and marshmallows with Mr. Saunders following with a pot of warm milk.

All hands immediately rose in the air. Nicole

watched in admiration at how hospitable Mr. and Mrs. Saunders were, considering there were currently fifteen crew members in their small home.

After everyone had been served a cup of hot chocolate and the perfect spot was chosen to film the older couple, Nicole got to work on touching up their hair and makeup.

"I love your perfume," Mrs. Saunders said as Nicole added a hint of color to her cheeks.

"Thank you. It's a scent I've been addicted to since high school."

"I can see why," she said with a smile. "It smells divine."

Nicole stopped what she was doing and pulled out a smaller bottle that she kept in her purse. "Here you go. I usually keep this on me. It's yours if you want it."

"I couldn't possibly take this," she said. "It's your favorite."

"Which means I can get more anytime." Nicole placed the small bottle in Mrs. Saunders's hand. "Please, keep it."

Her face lit up. "Thank you. You're such a sweetheart."

"You're welcome." Nicole went back to the task at hand.

"Are you dating anyone?" Mrs. Saunders asked.

"Um." *Well, technically no? Or technically yes?* Based off the conversation she'd had with Kendrick last night, she felt like the answer was yes, but since they were surrounded by coworkers, she replied no.

"That's interesting," Mrs. Saunders said. "I have a feeling you may be dating soon."

"Why do you think that?" Nicole asked as she placed light shadow on the woman's eyes.

"For starters, that young man in the corner of my living room is staring a hole through you right now." Nicole discreetly peeked over her shoulder and found Kendrick watching her closely.

"Kendrick, the creative director," Nicole said. "He and I are good friends."

"I bet that's not all you are," Mrs. Saunders said as she raised her eyebrows intuitively. "And if not, I can tell that he wants to be more than friends."

"How can you tell?" Nicole asked.

Mrs. Saunders glanced back over in Kendrick's direction. "When you all walked in here, his eyes were on you when introductions were made. When you went to this part of the room to pull out your makeup case, he watched you. Observed you. As if he were trying to make sure you didn't need anything." Nicole's stomach swarmed with butterflies at Mrs. Saunders's observations.

"And take right now for example," she said. "His mind seems cluttered by something, but he can't keep his eyes off you. Perhaps he doesn't know how to handle his feelings for you. Or he knows how to handle them, he's just contemplating his next move. No matter what other things may be consuming his thoughts right now, I think it's safe to say that you're at the top of that list."

Nicole shivered. "I can't believe you saw all that in the short amount of time that we've been here."

"She's probably noticed more than that," Mr. Saunders chimed in. "She's been intuitive since the day I met her." He reached over and squeezed his wife's hand, the action melting Nicole's heart.

"She's right, you know," Mr. Saunders said. "That boy's smitten as a kitten. He can't take his eyes off you." Nicole was sure her face looked flushed. She hadn't even known Mr. Saunders had been listening to the conversation.

"I'm pretty smitten with him too," she said honestly.

Mrs. Saunders looked from her husband to Nicole. "We know, sweetie. We know."

"Okay, everyone, let's get started," Nick said, interrupting her conversation with the Saunderses.

Nicole leaned toward the couple. "Thank you for sharing a piece of yourselves with me today."

The next hour of filming went by smoothly in large part to Mr. and Mrs. Saunders's authentic view on the true meaning of love. They even went into the history behind Valentine's Day and how Mr. Saunders had proposed on Valentine's Day sixty-five years ago.

"I met my wife when I sold her that very couch that still sits in our den today," Mr. Saunders said. "Back when we were engaged, folks weren't waiting a year or more before getting married. A month after I proposed, we were married. A year later, we'd given birth to our first of five kids. You see, we didn't go into our marriage with any plan or guideline. We had our own parents' marriages to look at as an example, but we also knew that no one relationship was the same. The world around us was constantly changing, forcing people to adapt in ways the generation before hadn't had to do. The key in surviving life's obstacles and building a strong marriage is sacrifice. You must be willing to make sacrifices for your love. For your family. For your future. Doing anything less is not an option."

Mrs. Saunders kissed her husband on the cheek after his speech. *It must be amazing to have a love that strong.* It occurred to Nicole halfway through filming with the Saunderses that she'd never had a love like theirs. She'd never dated a man who was willing to build a future with her and embark on a marriage or journey. To do this, one must realize that mistakes would be made, but as long as they were making them together and learning from them, that was the key to success.

"Anything else you want to share about your thoughts on true love?" the producer asked.

"My husband and I have learned our fair share of lessons, and even at our age, there is still more for us to learn. We've been married for sixty-five years. We have raised five kids, twelve grandkids and been fortunate enough to meet six great-grandkids."

Instead of looking at her husband or the cameraman as instructed, Mrs. Saunders looked around at the people in her living room before continuing. "Love may only be a four-letter word, but it holds a power that is much stronger than the curves of its letters. When we got married all those years ago, we had no idea what journey life would take us on. That day, we made a promise to one another by exchanging the most sacred of vows, and even today, we still look at one another in that same special way we did on our wedding day. The key to building a happy life is to realize that together, you can overcome any obstacles life throws your way. As we sit before you today discussing our journey as a couple, we celebrate the people we were… The people we are… And the people we have yet to become. United, we created a beautiful life built on the foundation of our love, and that's all that really matters."

Mrs. Saunders turned to her husband. "Can you believe we've been sharing a sofa together for over sixty-five years?"

Mr. Saunders placed a kiss on his wife's hand. "And I can't imagine sharing my favorite cushion with anyone else."

"And cut," Nick said in soft voice. Minutes after he'd made the announcement, the entire room was still silent, each lost in his or her own thoughts. Nicole could barely move after listening to such a powerful testament about love. The couple's words didn't just resonate with her. They touched her at her core, filling her veins with hope, promise and longing. To have someone love you so much—so unconditionally—was truly one of the few things Nicole craved most in the world.

"That was beautiful," someone finally said, breaking the silence. Similar sentiments were expressed around the room.

Mrs. Saunders caught Nicole's eye and smiled before tilting her head to the side. Nicole followed the tilt of her head and landed her eyes on Kendrick. The look she saw in his eyes stole her breath. *Hope. Promise. Longing.* His eyes reflected the same emotions she felt in her heart. The same feelings that she wanted so badly to share with a person she could fall in love with.

You could fall in love with him...you know it's true. When she'd made a promise to guard her heart, she hadn't ever thought that she'd meet a man like Kendrick, who'd make her doubt everything she thought she knew about love between a man and woman.

He began walking toward her, a purpose in his steps that others may not have noticed, but she definitely did.

"I have a bottle of champagne in my room and was thinking about ordering room service tonight," he said. "Is there any chance you can join me?"

She studied his eyes, her mouth growing dry from nervousness. It wasn't that he had said or done anything that should make her nervous, but being around a man who exuded sex appeal more than any man she'd ever met was enough to make her excited and anxious all at the same time.

"Yes," she finally said. "I'd love to join you tonight."

He smiled in that sly way that she was beginning to get attached to. *Nicole, you're falling faster than you realize.*

What had started as her trying to get to know Kendrick better was turning out to be a lot more than she'd bargained for, which begged the question... Was she falling in love or had she already fallen?

Chapter 11

Kendrick glanced around his hotel room for the tenth time. He'd never been the type to have nervous energy; however, as he waited for Nicole to knock on his door, that's precisely what he had.

Get ahold of yourself, Burrstone. This wasn't his first time inviting a woman back to his room. *But this is the first time in a while that you've invited a woman into your life who you like as much as you like Nicole.*

All day, he'd been thinking about her. Wanting to talk to her and continue the conversation they'd started last night. And listening to Mr. and Mrs. Saunders talk about the true meaning of love had really spoken to him. His grandparents had had a marriage like that before his grandmother had passed away, but hearing the older couple recount why they loved the other made him realize just how badly he wanted a type of love like that in his life.

Don't forget what happened last time. Even as the thought entered his mind, he knew it wasn't possible for him to forget what he'd been through with his ex. Even now, when he thought about her, it took more effort to remember the good times than the bad.

A knock on the door interrupted his thoughts. He took one more final glance around before he opened the door. *Damn.* There stood Nicole wearing a pair of high-waisted jeans that were slowly becoming his kryptonite, and a white tank. A beautiful rose quartz necklace hung from her neck, and her curls were pulled high atop her head. The sight before him was so beautiful, he didn't even hear her speak until he noticed her mouth was moving.

"I'm sorry, what did you say?"

She laughed. "I asked if you were going to let me in or would you rather I stay out in the hallway."

"I'm sorry," he said, stepping away from the door. "Please come in." As she walked past him, he breathed in her hypnotizing scent.

"What is the scent that you wear?" he asked.

"It may sound crazy," she said, "but I've mixed together two scents that I love to make this scent. I even package it up in small bottles when I travel."

"Doesn't sound crazy to me," Kendrick said as he motioned for to sit at the dining table. "Especially if doing so results in that delicious fragrance."

Nicole smiled over her shoulder before sitting down. "Wow, dinner looks amazing."

"They just brought it up, so it's still hot. I wasn't sure what you wanted, so I went with some good old-fashioned steak and potatoes."

Nicole sniffed the air. "It smells really good, and you can never go wrong with steak and potatoes."

"How amazing was it listening to the Saunderses today," Nicole said after they had begun to dig into their food.

"The love that they have for one another is so strong, but I think what stood out to me the most is the fact that they were willing to share their struggles and the lessons they learned along the way," Kendrick said.

"That's true. They didn't care that we were filming and that thousands of people would see the documentary. They were authentically themselves, and the producers encouraged them to be themselves."

"The rawness in their part of the documentary is going to shine through and inspire many to want to have the type of the relationship they have." *Present company included.* Kendrick met Nicole's gaze and wondered if she was thinking the same thing he was.

They ate the rest of the dinner in comfortable silence. When they'd almost finished their food, it occurred to Kendrick that he'd never been so relaxed around a woman that he didn't even need to talk to connect.

When dinner was over, he followed her lead and walked to the couch. "You must have a suite," Nicole said. "My room isn't this big."

"Yeah, it's a suite, but to be honest, I didn't need all this space. It feels better now that you're here."

She playfully hit him on the shoulder. "You're just saying that."

"I'm being serious," he said. "I couldn't wait to get you alone tonight. I thought about you the entire day... even more when the Saunderses were doing their documentary."

Her eyes widened. "You did?"

"Yeah, I did." He slid closer to her on the couch. "I had my eyes on you all day. According to Monty, I was bordering on *creepy stalker dude*."

Nicole's laugh echoed across the walls. "You didn't look creepy. I didn't even notice that you were looking at me until Mrs. Saunders pointed it out."

"I assumed you guys were talking about me when Mr. Saunders pulled me to the side after we finished shooting."

"Really? What did he say?"

Kendrick smiled as she remembered Mr. Saunders's words. "He said when I was old and gray, my biggest regret would be the chances I didn't take."

Nicole nodded in agreement. "My gran told me something similar on the phone yesterday morning. I let her words sink in during my entire flight to Lake Tahoe."

"I haven't stopped thinking about Mr. Saunders's words since he pulled me aside," Kendrick said. "We only talked for a short time, but there was so much power in his words. As we left their home, I made a promise to myself right then and there." He brought his hand to Nicole's cheek, lifting her mouth so that it was aligned to his.

Her eyes grew dark with desire and her breathing quickened. "What did you promise yourself?"

His eyes dipped to her lips as the memory of how talented she was with those passionate weapons hit him at his core. "I promised myself that when it came to you, I was taking all the chances I could get."

At her gasp, he covered her mouth with his and lifted her off the couch so that she was straddling him. She kissed him with the same urgency that he felt as her hands wrapped around the back of his neck, pulling him even closer to her.

His hands started on her back and slowly slid down to her butt cheeks, gripping them in his palms. When Nicole started rotating her hips, Kendrick held on, matching her thrusts even though they were still fully clothed.

"Kendrick," she said in between kisses, "I don't know how much more I can take."

"Me neither." He moved to her neck and collarbone, nipping her skin as he did. "Are you sure?" he asked, to make sure she wanted this just as much as he did.

"Yes," she said breathlessly. "I want this." She brought her lips back up to his. With no further confirmation needed, he lifted her from the couch and walked over to the bed. Once there, he gently laid her on top of the sheets, only breaking the kiss so that he could remove her jeans.

"In case I've never told you, I love how you look in high-waisted jeans," he said as he began tugging them down her thick thighs.

"I'm glad," she said with a smile. "Because they're my favorite."

"You know what I think my favorite will be?" He reached for the edge of her tank, pulling it slowly off her head.

"What?"

He stepped back to stare at her in her sexy teal lace bra and panty set. *She has more tattoos.* He counted two; each one was beautifully designed and looked perfect on her body. He forced himself not to bite his fist to keep from groaning. "Either you in a sexy bra and panty set." His eyes made their way to hers. "Or nothing at all."

She arched her back off the bed at his words. "Then I guess you better get me in nothing at all and see."

Insert fist bite now. Kendrick touched her bra straps, anxious to free the beautiful globes that he'd been drooling over since he first saw them straining in her crop top. When her nipples popped free, he froze.

"Are those…"

"Nipple rings," she said sheepishly. "Yeah, they are."

"Shit," he said, leaning closer to her breasts. *Sexiest. Shit. Ever.* Kendrick was never one of those superstitious types who believed in not going on the wrong side of the pole, or bad luck if you broke a mirror, or never walking underneath a ladder. Yet, as he stood there staring at Nicole's pierced nipples, he knew that it would be an absolutely *cruelty* if he didn't give her breasts his undivided attention.

He flicked his tongue over one nipple before flicking his tongue over the other. Once again, her back lifted off the bed, her sweet moans filling his ears as he sucked one nipple completely into his mouth.

Unable to continue fondling her breasts without fondling something else too, he slid her panties off, his fingers finding her sex with expert precision.

"Kendrick…" her voice trailed off.

"I'm far from finished bringing you pleasure," he said between licks.

She grabbed a pillow and squeezed it so hard that a few feathers popped out from the side. Kendrick didn't care what she did to handle the onslaught of pleasure he was bringing to her, as long as she knew that the beast in him was now unlocked and he wasn't going back into his cage anytime soon.

Her moans grew louder, proving that she was close to the edge of an orgasm. He switched to her other nipple to give it the same amount of attention as his fingers increased their pressure on her sweet spot.

Nicole's entire body erupted in an orgasm so strong, he had to grip her hips to keep her in place and make sure she didn't fall. *Is there anything that the woman does that isn't sexy as hell?* He had a feeling that answer was *no*. Once she started coming back down to reality, her eyes met his.

"As much as I enjoyed that," she said, her eyes running up and down his body, "I need you naked and inside me…*now*."

Kendrick didn't have to be told twice. He removed his shirt first, pulling it over his head and tossing it to the side.

"Oh, my," she said as she sat upright in the bed.

"Your tattoos are pure artwork…" She reached out a hand to touch one of his favorites. The lion on his bicep. "Why the lion?"

Kendrick glanced at it. "Because a lion represents strength, pride, leadership… It was a reminder that I have all the qualities instilled in me needed to leave my mark in this world."

"I love it," she said. "How many tattoos do you have?"

"Nine," he said as he unbuttoned his pants. "What about you? I love how intricate your designs are."

"I have five," she said, her eyes focused on his shaft, straining against his boxers."

"Hmm, I only counted two," Kendrick said. "I guess that means I have to do a thorough perusal of your body to find the others."

Nicole smiled slyly. "The others are on the other side of my body, so I guess you're right. You need to explore more."

Kendrick dropped his boxers, glad to be completely rid of his clothes. Apparently, he wasn't the only one glad that he was naked.

Nicole rose on her knees, her breasts gaining his interest again. When he went to touch them, she backed away and turned on all fours, her backside in full display for him to see. *Found the others*, he thought as he outlined each one with the tip of his fingers.

Once he was finished, Nicole turned her head over her shoulder. "Are you just going to admire me from behind or give me what I want?"

Kendrick raised an eyebrow. "I figured you'd want

to take it slow this first time," he said as he protected them both and joined her on the bed.

"When will you learn," she teased. "I like to do everything fast."

"You don't say," he said as he slowly slid his tip into her. "Then just because I'm in a playful mood, how about we take this slow."

Her protest died on her lips as he slowly pushed every inch of himself into her core.

"Ahh," she moaned, meeting his slow strokes.

Maybe going slow wasn't such a good idea, he thought. Going slow meant he felt every single vaginal muscle wrap and clench his length. It meant he felt the joining of their bodies in every part of his. Going slow meant that no matter how much he tried to keep his emotions in check when it came to Nicole LeBlanc, he was losing on all counts.

I don't know how much more I can take, she thought as Kendrick continued to stroke her painstakingly slowly. True, they weren't in a rush, but she wasn't sure her heart could handle how many feelings he was evoking within her right now.

He rolled his hips, going even deeper inside her. *How does he even have more to push in?* She'd been with well-endowed men before, but there was something about the impressive size and length of Kendrick that had her panting loudly. She just hoped Kendrick's room wasn't near any members of the crew because she was sure her moans were waking the entire floor.

When she'd first arrived at Kendrick's room, she

knew the night would result in sex. She'd been prepared mentally and physically for whatever the night would bring. However, she hadn't known that he would take his time with her body the way that he was. While Nicole liked to live in the fast lane, she was noticing that Kendrick liked to do everything slow and precise. *Just like he's doing with these languid strokes right now.*

She wasn't even sure it was possible, given how much she wanted him, but he'd somehow managed to get her even wetter than she was before.

"I'm close," she huffed, satisfied that he finally increased his movements. The slow buildup followed by the quickened pace was pushing her over the edge faster than she'd planned. Typically, it took a while for a man to make her orgasm through sexual intercourse. *Not with Kendrick.* He was single-handedly changing the way she viewed so many of the men she'd been with in the past.

And even though she couldn't see his body because he had her butt high in the air and her face was buried in the pillows, just imagining his scrumptious tattooed body only increased her pleasure.

"I'm right there with you, baby," he finally said. She breathed a sigh of relief that she wouldn't have to hold out much longer.

"Me too," she repeated seconds before she released another strong orgasm.

"Nicole," Kendrick said as he followed her over the edge of the orgasmic cliff. Nicole couldn't ever recall having an orgasm that close to a man before, but as hers was ending and his was beginning, the proximity of their orgasms caused the pleasurable relief to last even longer.

Kendrick collapsed on the bed, pulling her to his side and into his embrace. "That was…" his voice trailed off.

"I know," she said, still convulsing from the aftereffects.

Kendrick kissed her passionately before he curled his head into her neck. She smiled. *He's a cuddler…* The one thing that Nicole always liked doing after sex was cuddling, but she'd been with people in her past who didn't like to touch afterward. She was still smiling as she drifted off to sleep.

Chapter 12

The moonlight from the window caused Nicole to stir and awaken. For a few seconds, she wasn't sure where she was. Then she felt the strong arm draped across her midsection and remembered. *I slept with Kendrick last night.* She glanced at the clock on the nightstand. *I guess more like a few hours ago.*

Sex with Kendrick had been more than she'd ever expected and even with a few hours to sleep it off, she was still in awe of everything that had happened. *Be careful, Nicole... You already know he's the type of man who could break your heart.* It wasn't that she wanted to ignore the feelings she was beginning to have for Kendrick, but she did want to keep things in perspective. For starters, she couldn't forget why she'd come to California in the first place. Taking this job and embarking on a new opportunity had been a scary move to make, but one that she'd made for the main purpose of continuing her soul-searching journey.

But what if Kendrick fits into that journey? What if you were meant to meet him with the possibility of you both becoming more? After all, they were approaching the most romantic day of the year, and if love didn't find you on Valentine's Day, then, when would it?

Love? Girl, have you lost your mind? Admitting she was starting to have strong feelings for Kendrick was one thing, but love was another entity, entirely. She'd heard stories about couples falling in love after only a few days or weeks of knowing one another, but was that real love? Was that the kind of love that could withstand all obstacles like the Saunderses had mentioned?

Oh course it isn't, she thought. *And having this conversation with yourself is pointless since there is no way you're falling in love with Kendrick.* She glanced over her shoulder at the sleeping man next to her. *Except, what if I am falling in love with him? What if we're meant to be one of those stories for the ages that people repeat and tell others because they can't believe that a couple fell in love that fast?*

What if this entire time, she'd only dated those jerks to prepare her for the love of a real man like Kendrick? *What if? What if? What if?*

"Unless you're trying to go for round two, you should be asleep, beautiful."

Nicole jumped at the sound of his voice. "You scared me."

"That's because you were in deep thought." Kendrick propped his head on his elbow. "What's going on in that beautiful head of yours?"

Nicole turned to face him and mirrored his position. "I was thinking about the fact that we have to get up in a few hours and pack up to leave this beautiful place."

"I know. I'm not ready to leave either." Kendrick studied her eyes. "Are you sure that's all? What else is on your mind?"

That's another thing, she thought, laughing to herself. *He actually cares about how I feel.* "You're different from any man I've met before," she said. "In a good way."

Kendrick smiled. "That's good to know, although, I get the feeling that you've dated some real jerks in the past."

"More than I wish to divulge," she said. "But I guess the biggest jerk I've dated before is a guy who technically wouldn't even be considered a jerk."

"What do you mean?" Kendrick asked. "Did he disguise his true colors in the beginning?"

"Something like that," Nicole said as she thought back. "I met Marcus when I was a teenager, and we immediately got along. Back then, I was a bit of a tomboy and involved with every sport imaginable, but for some reason, Marcus only saw the girlie sides of me. Unlike some of the other boys in our high school class, he made me feel beautiful... Wanted... Included."

"What every high school student desires," Kendrick said.

"Exactly, and back then, he made me feel loved and

appreciated during a time when love and appreciation were scarce in my personal life."

"Your parents?"

"Yeah. My mom is in the military, and my dad was an army husband. That's the reason I've lived in so many places."

Kendrick nodded in understanding. "Was? Is your dad still living?"

"Yeah, he is." Nicole sat upright on the bed and pulled the sheet to her chest. "He walked out on us when I was thirteen and never looked back. From what I've found on social media, he has two kids now with his new wife."

"Damn," Kendrick said. "He never kept in contact with you?"

"Nope. Bottom line is that he couldn't handle being married to someone in the military. So instead of taking me with him, he just left me at home by myself with a letter saying that he was sorry and needed more."

Kendrick lightly touched her hand. "I'm sorry to hear that. My dad was never around either, so I understand. But it still sucks."

"It does," she said. "And at the time, I couldn't even get in contact with my mom, so after a week on my own, I realized he wasn't coming back and I called my grandparents. They picked me up, and I stayed with them until I was an adult."

"Your mom didn't come back?"

Nicole glanced out the window at the moon. "She claimed that she was too busy to deal with my dad, and me, for that matter. So she told me I was going to permanently live with my grandparents. She filed for divorce and went back to work with two less burdens to deal with… Her marriage and her daughter." She could still see the look of relief on her mother's face.

"After that, I went on a reckless path of trying to find love wherever I could. Don't get me wrong, my grandparents were amazing and loving, but I couldn't get past the feeling of not being wanted. I mean, how could a parent—or in my case two parents—wake up one day and say, 'Sorry, I don't want any parenting responsibility anymore. Please proceed to option B.'"

"Except there is no option B," Kendrick said. "Some parents don't realize the effect that their actions have on their children."

"Yup. And for me, option B came in the form of Marcus Hayes. I thought that as long as I had his love, I would be okay. The problem with putting all your love and faith into one person is that you deem the person worthy of such a gift."

"Judging by the look on your face, Marcus wasn't worthy."

"He wasn't," she said. "But I didn't see it at first. Like I said, he understood me and made me feel special. Everyone was friends with Marcus, and he had one of those infectious smiles and great personalities that meant that people always flocked to him."

"So from your perspective, being in love with someone who was so well liked by others validated that he was worth your love and affection too."

"Yeah, it was. Whenever he had a problem, I was right there by his side. It wasn't until I started having even more issues with my mom that I realized he wasn't offering the same advice and support I had given to him. It was almost like he had a Rolodex of ways he could pretend to be there for me without having to put forth the effort that I had exuded for him.

"But Marcus wasn't just my boyfriend. He was my best friend, so in turn, I latched on to everything about him. My opinions about certain things would change to what he thought. I liked the same things he liked. Did the same activities he did. Hell, I even entered college majoring in the same thing he majored in because I was convinced it was the type of career I wanted to pursue too."

Kendrick adjusted himself on the bed. "But you realized that it wasn't."

"Not even a little. Do you remember when I said that everyone who rocks with you may not always be for you?"

"Of course."

"Well, that was Marcus. He was a good guy. Still is. He was positive. Upbeat. Funny as hell and always made people laugh. I know that he cared about me and he valued our friendship, but I didn't realize that in trying to be everything that I thought he wanted and needed, I'd completely lost sight of my individuality. I was no longer Nicole LeBlanc—the opinionated girl who walked to the beat of her own drum. I might as well have been a carbon copy of Marcus Hayes.

"And I can't really blame Marcus," Nicole said as she scooted closer to Kendrick on the bed. "I was the one who had put Marcus on a pedestal and somehow convinced myself that he was the love that I desired. He was the love I lost when my father left. He was the love I'd always craved from my mother. He was the love I'd always had with my grandparents. But more importantly, I loved Marcus in a way that I had never loved myself, and that was the true tragedy."

It was then that Nicole noticed that Kendrick was rubbing his thumb in small circles on her thigh. The gesture made her calm and horny all at the same time.

"When did you finally realize that you needed to end your relationship with Marcus?" Kendrick asked.

"That's the funny thing," Nicole said with a forced laugh. "From thirteen to almost thirty, I had surrounded myself with people who represented someone I wanted to be. Friends, exes, coworkers, family members. You name it. My relationship with Marcus had ended when we were back in high school, but we maintained our friendship through college. It was my friendship with Marcus that caused the most damage. In some ways, a friendship was more sacred to me back then. Even after relationships ended, I tended to be friends with my exes."

She looked Kendrick in the eye. "It wasn't until I was nearing my thirtieth birthday that I realized that although my life hadn't been perfect, before my parents divorced, I had so many dreams and aspirations of what I wanted to do with my life. Things I wanted to accomplish. Places I wanted to visit. After their divorce—or maybe even before—I'd lost my way. My identity. The reason I was put on this earth.

"I recall going to a self-help convention with a few

of my friends and for whatever reason, the words of the keynote speaker really stood out to me. She'd been through hell and back, overcoming adversity and obstacles to become the person she was. She asked one question that will always stick with me... What do you love about yourself? And if your first response was what you didn't love about yourself, then you needed to do some reevaluating."

"That's a powerful question," Kendrick said. "Was that the turning point for you?"

Nicole nodded. "It was, mainly because even a couple hours after the speech ended, I was still making a list of things I didn't like and that wasn't healthy. I truly believe that it's okay to meet people in your life who impact you for the better, and therefore you take a piece of them with you wherever you may go. The issue is when you can't authentically name any part of yourself that you love that wasn't influenced by someone else. I'd spent too long being scared to take chances and make mistakes. Not willing to change for fear of the unknown. I needed to make my own path. I needed to define my own journey and stop searching for love when I didn't love myself. So that's precisely what I did. The next day was the *first* day toward becoming a better me. Oh, and check this out." She left the bed and reached into her purse for a sheet of paper.

"What's this?" he asked as he opened the sheet of paper. Nicole held her breath as he took a good look at it. "Is this a tattoo design?"

She laughed in surprise. "How did you know?"

"Because I know tattoos, and it seems to be something we have in common." Kendrick traced the design with his finger. "I love the curves of the infinity symbol intertwining in the flowers."

"They're sweet peas," she said. "My grandparents used to always call me sweet pea, and my grandmother still does. I'm not an artist by any means, so this is just a rough sketch of the next tattoo I want. Hopefully, I can get it while I'm in LA."

That's right...you have to go back to Miami soon. The words were a little bitter, even in his mind.

"If you're trying to get the tattoo in LA, I actually know the perfect shop. A friend of mine owns the spot, and even though he's normally really busy, I'm sure he'll fit you in as a favor to me."

"I would love that," Nicole said. "Especially since this tattoo is something that I've wanted for a while. I just haven't had the time to get it. It represents my journey so far, so it's really important to me."

Kendrick placed the sheet of paper on the nightstand and leaned closer to her. "You're amazing and your story is inspiring. I know that it's taken you a while to get here, but you're one of the most self-aware people I know."

"Thank you," she said with a smile. "I've actually never talked to anyone about my journey in as much detail as I have with you."

Kendrick flashed her a handsome smile. "I think you should be rewarded for your honesty."

"Oh, yeah?" She smirked. "What did you have in mind?"

He placed his hand on her chin and tilted it upward.

"I was thinking of starting with a kiss." He placed a soft kiss on her lips. "And another kiss." This time, he kissed her neck. "And another." He kissed the top of her breasts.

"For kicks, I was thinking of going even further." He trailed sweet kisses in between her breasts, down her stomach and to her thighs.

"What's a kiss without going for the gusto?" He placed a kiss onto her nub, slowly adding a little tongue. Nicole was already spreading her legs wider for him.

"Did you have a French kiss in mind?" she asked.

"Always," he said, then proceeded to show her just the kind of French kiss he meant.

Chapter 13

Nicole breathed in the fresh beach air as she walked along the Venice Boardwalk with Kendrick. Well, it wasn't exactly fresh. It was more like beach water, mixed with stale pizza, and random incense that was burning in almost every store they passed. Regardless, she was enjoying her first time on the boardwalk.

They'd arrived back to LA three days ago, and since his mom was in town assisting with renovations for his home and Nicole was on Bare Sophistication duty, they'd only briefly seen each other when they were in the studio shooting the last commercial.

Their time in Lake Tahoe had been amazing, and if they hadn't been there for work, Nicole had no doubt that they would have stayed longer. Though she hadn't gotten a chance to corner Angelica, judging by the lovey-dovey looks her and Monty were exchanging in the shuttle on the way to the airport, she'd say they probably shared the same sentiments.

"It's a few stores down," Kendrick said as they neared his friend's tattoo shop. The day after they'd landed in LA, she'd called Kendrick to take him up on his offer of having his friend do her tattoo. He'd surprised her when he mentioned that he'd already put in a call to his friend and that today he was available due to a cancellation.

"Here we are," Kendrick said as he held open the door. Nicole immediately stopped when she walked through the door.

"I thought you said he wasn't busy?" She looked around at all the waiting patrons.

"They aren't here for my friend Ant," Kendrick said. "Ant owns the shop, but he has six other artists who work with him. He only takes the high-profile clients now in the private rooms in the back."

Nicole followed Kendrick down the long hall to the back of the shop that had another door. "Follow me," he said, opening the door.

"Well, if it isn't KD," a muscular tattooed man said when they walked through the door.

"What's up, Ant?" Kendrick dapped fists with the man before turning to Nicole. "When I first walked in this shop, my mom and I had just moved to LA. When I wasn't working at my uncle's winery, I was here at the shop."

"One of the best prodigies I ever had," Ant said. "When this dude told us he was trading in his tattoo equipment for a life in Hollywood, we hated to lose a good artist, but couldn't be anything but happy for him. Plus, he still tattoos when he wants. We keep a spare room open for him."

Nicole's eyes widened. "You never told me that you actually used to do the tattoos. Only that you would design them."

Kendrick shrugged. "When I first walked into this shop, I'd only had the intention of showing a few of my drawings."

"Until we schooled him that only true tattoo artists tat their own creations," Ant said. "But the kid had a certain energy about him that I liked. So I offered to teach him a few things. Next thing you know, he was booking his own clients and renting one of our rooms."

"Helped me pay my way through film school," Kendrick said. "And it kept me off the streets."

Nicole glanced at Kendrick. "You're amazing," she said.

"Thanks. You're pretty amazing too." He was looking at her so intently that it took all her energy not to squirm under his gaze.

"How do you two know one another?" Ant asked.

Nicole noticed a flash of hesitance in Kendrick's eyes before he responded. "Uh, we currently work together on those Valentine's Day commercials and documentary I was telling you about. Nicole is a makeup artist and hairstylist with the agency."

Ant lifted an eyebrow. "You work together?" He wasn't so much asking as he was repeating what Kendrick had said.

"Yeah." A silent communication seemed to pass between Ant and Kendrick. Although Nicole didn't know what it was about, she figured it had something to do with the reason Kendrick had that rule about not dating people he worked with. *Eventually, you're going to have to ask him more about that.*

"She knows about my rule," Kendrick said, breaking her thoughts. His eyes held hers. "Believe it or not, I knew the day she walked in the studio that I wouldn't be able to stay away. Sometimes, you meet someone who makes you question all the preconceived notions you once had. That's what Nicole does to me. She shows me a different side of things."

She relaxed under his warm gaze. In all honesty, they'd moved so far beyond being coworkers that she'd forgotten that they did work together.

"So," Ant said. "Are you two gonna stand there staring at one another all intense and shit, or are you going to tell me why you're here?"

"Right." Kendrick laughed. "Remember I called and said a friend needed a favor? We're here because Nicole was hoping that she could get you to do a tattoo for her. It's actually her own design, but it needs some tweaking before she gets it done." Kendrick pulled the piece of paper with her design on it from his back pocket and handed it to Ant.

"Cool design," Ant said. "Does it have a meaning?"

"It does," Nicole said. "It represents strength, resilience. It's a reminder of how far I've come on my personal journey and how much further I still have to go. More importantly, it's a reminder to always love myself…flaws and all."

Ant glanced from Nicole to the paper. "I like it," he said as he handed the paper back to Kendrick. "KD, I think you need to take this one."

Kendrick's eyes widened. "Nah, man. I haven't done a tat in a while. This is special to Nicole, so she needs the best."

"Man, you know you're extremely talented. Besides, I taught you everything you know, so you're as good as me."

Ant looked back at Nicole. "What do you say? Do you trust my man to give you this tat?"

She studied Kendrick for any signs that he couldn't handle this. *He doesn't seem nervous about doing my tattoo. He seems more nervous about what my response will be.* Trusting someone to permanently ink your body wasn't a decision to be taken lightly. There were so many things that could go wrong. *But you're done being careful,* she reminded herself. So, if the question was if she trusted Kendrick with such a big task, the answer was easy.

"Yes," she said, her eyes not leaving Kendrick's. "I trust him…completely."

The relief she saw reflected in his eyes was quickly replaced with a look she couldn't interpret. *Intrigue? Surprise?* When he pulled her in for a sweet kiss, she realized what it was… *Appreciation.*

There were so many feelings coursing through his body, he knew he had to get it together so that he could get in tattoo mode. *She trusts me...* And not only was he amazed that she trusted him, but he was in awe at how confident she was in her conviction.

"Come on," Ant said. "I have a room set up already."

Kendrick observed his friend. "When you told me to bring in Nicole, was this your plan all along? You had to figure I was bringing her for a tattoo."

"Who, me?" Ant pretended to be surprised by the accusation. "Nah, man, you're giving me too much credit." Ant leaned closer so that Nicole wouldn't overhear. "But for real though, the minute she showed you the tat design, you were itching to make it your own and tattoo her. Am I right?"

Kendrick glanced over his shoulder at Nicole and caught her smile. "Yeah, you're right," he said. "I just didn't think she'd trust me with something so sacred to her."

"I studied her first," Ant said. "Watched to see how you two interacted. Y'all had a good vibe and energy together. Although seventy percent of folks come to the shop with the intention of getting a tat, the other thirty percent are nervous and hesitant about the decision. You and I both know that making the client comfortable enough to ink their body is half the battle." Ant's voice got lower. "And I don't know what changed your mind about dating someone you work with, but I like her, man. She's a good one."

Kendrick heard the words that Ant didn't say. "Thanks, man. She caught me off guard, but in so many ways, she reminded me that I couldn't let my past affect my future."

Ant slapped him on the back of the shoulder. "I'm proud of you, man."

When they walked into the room where Kendrick would be tattooing Nicole, he immediately felt at home. *I missed this place.* There was a time when the shop had been like a second home to him. In a few ways, it still was.

"I forgot to ask," Kendrick said when Ant had stepped away. "Where do you want this tattoo?"

"On the side of my hip," she said. "I know it will hurt like hell, but it's the perfect spot for this tat."

Kendrick's mind immediately began racing with ideas of how to enhance the tattoo for her hip. "I already have ideas brewing." He handed her a sheet. "Why don't you remove your pants and panties, but keep on your shirt. Do you want me to step out?"

Nicole glanced at the curtain separating their room from the hallway. "Would you lose your professional card if you stayed here while I changed?"

"No," he said with a laugh.

"Then stay." She kicked off her gym shoes one foot at a time. When her hands went to her leggings, she had his undivided attention. She slid the cotton material slowly down her thighs in a way that made his hands itch to touch her.

Once she'd finished removing her leggings, she ran her thumbs along the edge of her lilac panties, playing with the delicate straps.

"There are no cameras in here in case you were wondering."

Nicole smirked. "I wasn't worried. I figured you would have stopped this if there were."

"You damn right," he said with more force than he intended. He was the only one allowed to see her naked. Point-blank.

She finally slid her panties down her legs, kicking them to the side to join her leggings. His eyes locked on the part of her he'd gotten very acquainted with a couple days ago. *She's beautiful.* Nicole was one of those types of women who knew she was gorgeous, but didn't flaunt her beauty around. She was real. Honest. *And you're falling for her quicker than you realize.*

It didn't surprise him that he was developing strong feelings for Nicole. It had been a long time since he'd fallen in love with a woman, but he knew he was falling in love with her.

Unable to resist himself, he walked over to her and squeezed her butt cheeks, pulling her closer to him. She let out a small gasp when she felt how hard he was. He wasn't ashamed to let her see the effect she was having on him. If anything, he'd rather she know exactly where he stood so that she wouldn't be shocked if there came a point where he couldn't hold back his feelings anymore.

"If I don't release you right now, you're never getting this tattoo," he said.

"Fine." She grinned. "I've been waiting years to get this tattoo so you better get to work."

As Kendrick began drawing the intricate design with the infinity symbol and sweet peas, he was reminded of why he loved tattoos so much. It was a freedom of expression that he didn't get from much else. Although he had given the tattoo design his own trademark, he also kept the design in line with Nicole's other tattoos, making it authentically her.

After the drawing was complete, he helped her to a nearby chair and covered her with the white sheet, only leaving her right hip exposed. He put on gloves before he applied the design to her skin, then traced the outline of the design with a red marker. Thirty minutes later, the design was complete.

"I've been thinking about the perfect way to enhance this drawing ever since you showed it to me," he said. "Here, let me help you up so you can see it." Kendrick led her to the floor-length mirror. "Based off everything you said to me when we were in Lake Tahoe, I feel as though this design represents the statement you're trying to make. What do you think? Do you like it?"

"No," she said, placing her hand on his arm. "I more than like it. I'm in *love* with this design." She looked at him, her eyes gleaming with unshed tears. "Thank you so much."

"You're welcome," he said. When she leaned forward to hug him, he immediately pulled her into his embrace. Of all the tattoo designs that he'd ever created, this one meant more to him than he could express.

"But we're just getting started. Now comes the hard part." He helped her back in the chair and made sure she was as comfortable as she could be. He grinned when he noticed that the equipment was all the brands that he liked and was used to working with. *That guy*, he thought. Ant seemed like he wasn't one to play matchmaker, but that's precisely what he'd been doing.

Chapter 14

It took Kendrick longer than it normally would to set up, but he wanted everything perfect before he began Nicole's tattoo. "I'm going to start now. If at any time you want me to stop because it hurts, just let me know and I'll take a break. I'm thinking we need to do this in two sessions. The outline today and the color later."

"Okay," she said, taking a deep breath. "I'm ready."

Ten minutes into the tattoo, Kendrick realized that although Nicole may have gotten other tattoos before, she was experiencing how much more painful it was to get a tattoo on the hip bone.

"Can you talk to me?" she asked. "To take my mind off the pain."

"Sure," he said. "What do you want to talk about?"

"Hmm." She closed her eyes until he finished the

line he was tattooing. "Can you tell me why you created your rule about not dating people you work with?"

He glanced her way before continuing what he was doing. He knew it would come up sooner or later. "I created that rule because of what I'd gone through with two of my exes," he said. "With Veronica, I'd met her in film school, but we'd only been friends at the time. We ran into each other a couple years later when we were both vying for the same assistant director position. At the time, I think it meant more to her than it did to me, but I still really wanted the position. The hiring process was three months long, and I'd never applied for a job that had us go through so many trials before someone was chosen. In that time, Veronica and I grew even stronger and quickly started dating. Round after round, only her and I remained until finally they were ready to choose the winner. At this point, I thought I was in love with her, and I told her it didn't matter who got it."

"She got it?" Nicole asked. "Veronica got the job?"

"Nope, I got it. And after I accepted, we grew even closer and I moved into her place at her suggestion since it was in a nicer part of town. I dated her for two years before I realized she was only using me to further her own career. The day she landed a director role was the day that I should have been excited for her, but when I went home, I knew something was up. She sat me down and told me that now that she'd landed that position, she no longer needed me and I was holding her back from reaching her full potential."

"Man," Nicole said. "That's a tough pill to swallow."

"It was," he said. "I'd always been more of a serious dater than the player type, so I was completely caught off guard by what she'd told me. I'd spent thousands of dollars on this woman because she claimed she couldn't afford to pay her bills and rent. At the time, I didn't think to ask her how she'd been getting by before. I'd never met her parents, so I hadn't known she came from money and was cut off financially until she'd finished telling me that I was no longer wanted in her life and that she'd reconciled with her parents. She handed me a box of my belongings, then told my ass that I could pick up the rest the following week."

"That's crazy," Nicole said, shaking her head. "I would have given her a piece of my mind."

"I was upset for a long time, especially when new blogs and magazines released information about her dating a famous actor. But then when I thought more about it, all I could do was pity the poor soul who ended up with that gold digger and move on with my life."

Nicole was still shaking her head when he tightened the screws on the tattoo machine.

"You mentioned exes as in plural," Nicole said. "Who was your other ex who contributed to you creating the rule?"

"Amanda," he said, shaking his head. "I met Amanda back when we were kids and I was still living in Chicago. Back in the day, we used to be inseparable. We both got jobs sweeping the floors at a corner store in the neighborhood. Then, in our early teens, we both got a job stacking the fruit at a local grocery store. When we turned sixteen, we both got jobs at the mall at a popular shoe store. She was one of the good girls in the neighborhood. The one who everyone wanted to be around because she represented a purity that was rare in our community."

"So you two were really close friends?"

"Yeah. At least it started off that way." Kendrick thought back to when he first asked her to be his girlfriend. "Remember when I told you I was involved with the wrong stuff and crowd back then?"

"Of course."

"I guess you could say that in order to fit in, I had to do some things I wasn't proud of. As I've said before, my mom was prideful and she didn't want to ask her family for money, but financially, we were in trouble when the factory she worked at closed down. Since I wasn't making the amount of money I needed to make, I turned to other avenues, which meant I had to sell some things I'd rather not sell. Associate with people who I didn't necessarily want to be associated with, but did because it was better to keep your enemies closer. I've always been smart, and it wasn't until I'd had a serious eye-opening conversation with my grandparents that I realized the path I was headed down didn't fit me.

"When you're at the top of your game in the streets, everyone wants to be your friend. It's only when you start to want another life for yourself that things begin to fall apart. Then suddenly instead of having people who watch your back, you discover you're the only one watching it."

Nicole nodded. "We didn't go through the same situation, but I understand how you feel."

"It was tough," he said. "To want to be accepted by a crowd while at the same time wanting to stand alone. It was a weird place to be. Amanda was one of the people who had my back, but the minute I started wanting more, craving more, doing better in school so that I could raise my GPA and get into a good college, she didn't want to have anything to do with me. When I found out she was pregnant by one of my closest friends, it was around the same time my mom told me we were moving to LA. Even though I had family in LA, I hadn't wanted to leave Chicago. And the only time I'd seen my cousin Bryant was at family reunions, so he and I didn't share the bond we have now, back then. He was clean-cut around the edges, whereas I... I was..."

"You were more jagged..."

"Yeah, exactly. But despite what I wanted, I knew there wasn't a reason for me to stay in Chicago anymore. It will always be home, but I needed a change. To this day, I don't know if my mom was telling the truth when she said that she'd gotten an opportunity to work at an educational foundation in LA or if she saw the path I was headed down and was willing to do anything she could to redirect it."

"I know I only met your mom once," Nicole said, "but I bet she probably came to LA for you and maybe the job opportunity came shortly after."

"You're probably right," he said. "That was also the first time I'd seen my mom ask for help from a family member. Our first year in LA, we stayed at my uncle's winery."

"Did you ever see Amanda after you moved?" Nicole asked.

"I sure did," he said. "She moved to LA."

"She moved to LA?" Nicole said in surprise. "How did that happen?"

Kendrick adjusted his hand so that he could tattoo the lines of the sweet peas. "I'd just completed my first commercial with the agency when Bryant called and said she was at the winery. She knew that my uncle owned it, so it wasn't too surprising. I hadn't seen her in over twelve years at the time, and after that drama with Veronica, I was happy to see her. We decided to go out to dinner to catch up. She updated me on how folks were doing in the neighborhood, and we laughed at some of the crazy things we did as kids. It was like old times."

"Did she tell you why she was in LA that night?"

"Yeah, she did. My ex-friend and the father of her son had been in a bad accident and was paralyzed a year before. She said she'd been so distraught that her son was staying with her parents. I'd heard about it from someone I still kept in contact with from Chicago, but I'd thought they weren't together at the time. She told me that she'd moved to LA to pursue her dreams of becoming an actress and once she'd bettered herself, she would move her son here."

"Are you sure he isn't your son?" Nicole asked. "Given how everything went down between you both."

"I had a paternity test done when her son was born. He isn't my child."

"Oh, okay." Nicole adjusted her head on the reclined

chair. "So, the only thing she came to LA for was to become an actress? Nothing else?"

"If you're asking if she came to LA so that we could get back together, then that answer is yes. Amanda wasted no time apologizing and letting her intentions be known. I'd always had a weak spot for her because I'd known all the hardship and trouble she'd gone through. So within weeks, we'd fallen back into our old pattern and decided to try a relationship again. She moved into my place, and I welcomed her into my world. My mom couldn't stand her. They'd never gotten along. But everyone else liked being around her. Even Monty and Angelica developed a friendship with her. And her acting career took off, as well. Before I knew it, she was starring in independent films."

Nicole's eyes widened. "Is Amanda Mason your ex?"

"Yeah," Kendrick said. "You've seen her work?"

"I have. I'm a sucker for independent films. But didn't Amanda go to rehab a few years ago and then appear on two seasons of that rehab reality show?"

"She did. The first time she appeared on the show, we were together. I'd watched her go down a downward spiral the minute she began booking movies and shows. She began coming home late, and when she did, I could tell she was on drugs and drinking heavily. Then one day, she didn't come home. Days turned into weeks and weeks turned into an entire month. Then one day, I receive a random call from someone who rattles off the address of where she is. When I get there, I check out the house first. When I got to the back of the house, I saw her in the window having sex with another man."

"Oh, no." Nicole's hand flew to her mouth. "That's terrible."

"Even worse, she was so high at the time, she didn't even know who I was when I told her I'd come to take her home. I spent that car ride with her kicking and screaming for me to let her naked self out the car and me telling her to calm down. When we got home, I practically had to lock her in the bedroom until she fell asleep. I hadn't talked to Amanda's parents since she'd arrived in LA, so I called them, unsure of what else to do. That's when I learned that they had full custody of her son and hadn't spoken to their daughter in years."

"I had a feeling that may be the case," Nicole said in a soft voice. "I hate that you had to go through that."

"Me too," he said. "But as you've said, apparently it was a lesson I had to learn. Now I see what I failed to see all those years ago. For Amanda, it had never been about us as a couple or the love I had for her. It was all about the image she wanted to portray to the world. It was about what I could do for her and connecting her with the contacts I was making in the industry. I haven't seen her in two years, but last I heard, she was trying to get her acting career started again. And although I wish her the best, I could never go down that road again."

Nicole grew quiet.

"What's wrong?" he asked.

"Nothing. I was just thinking about how much we had in common. I know it shouldn't keep surprising me, but it does. You're so amazing, I just don't understand why you've had such bad luck in relationships."

"I could say the same about you," Kendrick said with a smile. "You haven't had the best of luck either. But meeting you has opened my eyes to more than I ever thought possible."

She tilted her head toward him. "And what's that?"

Kendrick let his eyes roam over her body as she lay on the reclined chair, stopping at her eyes. "I learned that despite the obstacles I've had to face, I still have a lot of love to offer a woman…the right woman… You helped me see that. Hell, you helped me see a whole lot more than just that, but opening up my heart to love again is definitely at the top."

He went back to tattooing her hip as she lay there, observing him. He was sure her brain was trying to process what he'd just said, and he hoped she understood one thing and one thing only. It may not be soon. It may even be months from now. However, one day, he was going to make her his, so she'd better be prepared when that time came.

Chapter 15

"You're going down," Monty yelled as he picked up his pool cue.

Nicole and Angelica laughed. "Do you have to say that every time you pick up the cue?" Angelica asked.

"Yes, I do," he said. "Otherwise, you might think I'm going to take it easy on you and let you win. Since that's not going to happen, I felt it best that I remind you how manly I can be."

"Yeah, babe. You're so manly." Angelica and Monty may have been doing their usual back and forth banter, but Nicole read between the lines.

They were all gathered at Kendrick's condo for pool night. The moment Nicole walked into his condo, she was taken aback by the gray, black and white decor. For the past few days, they'd been cooped up in her apartment, which wasn't exactly conducive to intimacy, considering Nicole shared an apartment with Kyra since they were there temporarily. After Kyra had walked in on them in the living room in an undressed state, Kendrick had suggested they go to his place even though it was farther into the city.

Once they'd arrived, Kendrick had forgotten that he and Monty had plans, so instead of making it a guys' night, Monty and Angelica had both come over for a night of pool instead.

"So, what's going on with you and Monty?" Nicole whispered when Monty was out of earshot. "We haven't gotten a chance to talk much since we got back from Lake Tahoe."

"That's because you and Kendrick have been in your own love cocoon," Angelica teased. "And the only reason I know that is because Monty and I have been in our own."

Nicole squealed. "I knew it."

"Hey," Monty said. "The least you can do if you two were going to talk about me while Kendrick gets food is to not make it so obvious."

"Sorry, babe," Angelica said. "I was just telling Nicole how great you are in the bedroom."

"Oh," Monty said as he stood a little taller. "If that's the case, then squeal away."

Nicole shook her head and turned her attention back to Angelica. "How do you feel? What does this mean? Are you officially dating? Is the sex really that amazing?"

Angelica laughed. "One, amazing. Two, we're still figuring that out. Three, yes. And four, hell, yes!"

"I'm so happy to hear that," Nicole said. "You two are great together."

"Thank you. It's been a long time coming. And speaking of being great together, how are things with you and Kendrick? You both haven't stopped smiling all night."

Nicole grinned. "Things with Kendrick are better than I've ever imagined. He's such a gentleman, but then again, he's also got that edgy swag that I can't help but drool over every time he walks into a room. I hate to say it, but it's almost like I'm waiting for something bad to happen because everything is so good."

"I know the feeling," Angelica said. "After my divorce, I swore that it was the last time I'd open up my heart to a man. I didn't expect to meet someone like Monty, who not only understands me, but has gone through the same heartache that I have."

"It's funny how that works," Nicole said. "When your heart is broken and you don't foresee yourself ever healing from the experience, you never imagine that you will find a partner who has undergone exactly what you have. We know that thousands of people experience heartache every day, but it doesn't stop us from being caught up in our own situation."

Angelica nodded. "Then suddenly, someone walks into your life and gives you a new perspective on love, and before you can pinpoint the exact moment that it happened, you're ready to open up your heart again."

"And risk it all for the possibility of embarking on

a once in a lifetime romance," Nicole finished. Both women grew quiet, each caught up in her own thoughts.

"The approaching holiday must be getting to us," Angelica said, breaking the silence.

"Either that, or these men have gotten us wrapped around their fingers."

"Shh," Angelica said, placing a finger in front of her lips. "Monty has ears like an elephant, so don't say that too loud."

"I heard every word," Monty said on cue. Both women laughed as Kendrick walked in with the food. *He still takes my breath away.* Tonight everyone was dressed casual and comfortable, so Kendrick was wearing black jogging pants and a white T-shirt. Simple, yet still sexy.

He walked over and placed a gentle kiss on her lips that quickly escalated to a more passionate one.

"Uh, did y'all forget we're here?" Monty asked.

"Just didn't care," Kendrick said.

"Yeah, we got that," Monty said. "Man, quit kissing Nicole and come take your turn." Giving her one last kiss, he grabbed the pool cue.

"Have you guys talked about his ex?" Angelica whispered.

"Which one? Veronica or Amanda?"

Angelica raised her eyebrows. "He told you about both of them? Wow, he must really like you."

"We've talked about some pretty serious topics, but I'm glad we did. I've opened up to him in ways I never have to any man before, and I think he feels the same way about me."

"What are you and Kendrick going to do about the fact that you live in Miami?" Angelica asked.

"I'm not sure," Nicole said with a sigh. "We're done filming in a few days, and we haven't even discussed the fact that in another week or so, we're closing up the Bare Sophistication pop-up and I'm going back to Miami."

"You need to talk about it," Angelica whispered. "I get the feeling that Kendrick expects you to stay, so if he hasn't brought it up, you should bring it up to him."

"How do I even bring that up?"

"Easy," Angelica said with a shrug. She glanced at the men to make sure they were still engrossed with the pool game before continuing. "I'd start with 'Kendrick, I'm falling for you and if you want to continue this relationship, I'd love to stay in LA for a while longer.'"

"I didn't even tell you I was falling for him."

"Girl, please." Angelica rolled her eyes. "It's written all over your face. Just like I'm sure how I feel about Monty is written all over mines. It's nothing to be ashamed of. Kendrick's a great guy, and Monty and I have waited years for him to find someone like you. And we don't want you to move back either. I'm not saying you have to uproot your life for a man, but based off our conversations, I know you love it here and wouldn't mind staying. Now that you guys have found one another, don't let fear hold you back."

Nicole looked at Kendrick, knowing that everything Angelica was saying was true. Even so, she was still nervous to tell him how she felt. *Just remember...no more being scared.* Regardless of how he felt about her, she owed it to herself to tell Kendrick how she really felt. Best-case scenario, he'd tell her that he felt the same way and ask her to stay in LA so that they could take their relationship even further. Worst-case scenario, she'd tell Kendrick how she felt only to realize that he wasn't feeling as strongly about her and as she was about him.

But even if that's the case, think about how much you've gained from being with a man like Kendrick…if even for a short time. Mind made up, she knew she had to open up. Exposing herself to rejection wasn't an easy thing to do, but she'd regret it even more if she went back to Miami having never shared her true feelings.

You're such a chicken. Monty and Angelica had been gone for a half hour, and Nicole still hadn't worked up enough courage to tell Kendrick how she felt.

All you have to do is get over your fear of starting the conversation. The words will just come after that. She'd been repeating the same thing in her mind since halfway through the pool game, but no matter how easy it sounded in her mind, saying it aloud was entirely different.

"Are you okay?" Kendrick asked as he gathered the empty cups and walked them over to the kitchen.

"I'm fine," she said as she followed him with the remaining buffalo sauce. "I just have a few things on my mind."

"Really? Can I help with anything?"

Yeah, you can tell me how you feel first and put me out of my misery. "No, not really," she said instead as she turned toward the refrigerator to place the sauce inside.

Chicken. That was your chance and you missed it! She froze. If she was going to agonize over it all night, she might as well just own up to her feelings and lay her heart on the line.

"Actually, I do have something to say." She turned around quickly, ready take full advantage of her new-found courage and slammed into Kendrick's chest.

"Oh, no," she said as the buffalo sauce went all over his white shirt and jogging pants. "I'm so sorry!" Ignoring the sauce that spilled on her clothes, she grabbed a towel and tried to help him clean it up only to slip on the spilled dip and fall on hard tile of the floor.

"I'm starting to see a pattern," Kendrick said with a laugh as he helped her up. "First the drinks in the bar. Now buffalo sauce in my condo? If you want my attention, all you have to do is ask."

"Ha-ha, very funny." She glanced down at her buf-falo-sauce-covered clothes. "I guess I just had my mind on something else."

Kendrick placed his hand under her chin. "Are you sure there isn't anything I can do to help ease that racing mind of yours?"

Nicole grinned. "Well, now that you mention it, I'd love to get out of these messy clothes."

His eyes sparked. "That can be arranged." Without warning, he bent down and lifted her into his arms. She squealed as her arms wrapped around his neck.

"Where are you going?"

"You'll see," he said as he walked up the stairs with

her still in his arms as if she weighed nothing at all. *Too sexy.* Once they were at the top, he carried her to the master bedroom, only putting her down once they were standing in front of the bathroom.

"How about we get you clean," he said as he cut on the light, revealing a breathtaking stand-up shower with a whirlpool tub in the corner of the bathroom.

"It's beautiful," she said, getting a closer look. "But you know I'm not supposed to get my tattoo wet. It's still healing."

"A little water won't hurt," he said. "Besides, I have a mist option, so you'll be fine."

"In that case," she said as she lifted her shirt over her head. "Let's get clean."

Kendrick shook his head, his eyes glued to her breasts. "I don't think I'll ever get used to seeing you naked. It hits me right in the gut every time."

"Flattery will get you everywhere." She removed his shirt next and then hers. Once they were both naked and the temperature of the water was perfect, they both stepped in the shower.

Before she could even get a good lather going on the washcloth he provided, he was already placing kisses along her spine.

"I thought the point was to get clean," she teased. Instead of stopping, he moved his kisses to her neck.

"I figured we could get dirty before we get clean." He ran his fingers along her side, the movement giving her goose bumps all over. It wasn't until she was squirming from his touch that she realized he was outlining the tattoo he'd done on her.

"I can't stop looking at it," he said. "I can't wait to finish the job."

She turned to face him. "I loved everything about the experience." She placed a kiss on his neck and was rewarded with an appreciative groan. *Will it always be like this?* she wondered. *One kiss. One touch. One look is all it takes to turn my heart to mush around him.* Even in her mind, she felt like she was sounding like a broken record, but in some ways, she still couldn't believe how their relationship had escalated.

She met his eyes. "Kendrick, I… I…" *Great, now I'm stuttering.* She was failing at this whole *tell him how you really feel* thing. Luckily, Kendrick decided to put her out her misery.

His lips collided with hers at the same time that he pushed her toward the bathroom wall. Unlike the soft kisses he'd been giving her all night, this kiss was all-consuming and touching her heart in ways it had never been touched.

Her thighs rose on their own accord into Kendrick's awaiting palms. Only then did she notice he'd managed to put on protection. *Oh, he's good.* The problem was, he wasn't just good at one thing. He was good at so many things, she could barely keep track anymore.

When she felt his shaft rub against her core, Nicole adjusted him so that he was positioned directly in front of her entryway. Slowly, he slid into her, both of them moaning as he did. Nicole closed her eyes. *I'll never get tired of how this feels.*

When he was buried deep within her, all she wanted was for him to be even deeper. Being with Kendrick just felt so right. It felt like she'd waited her entire life to experience a moment like this. It was pure unrestrained bliss, and she was loving every minute of it.

That's because you're in love with him. Her eyes opened and landed on his as the importance of this moment crashed over her in constant waves. Had she suspected she was in love with him? Yes. Did she suspect that he cared for her too? Definitely. Had she planned on telling him tonight that she wanted to stay in LA? For sure. Was she still surprised that now—with him buried inside her to the hilt—that the only word floating around in her mind began with an *L*, ended with an *E* and was four letters? Damn right she was.

Being in love with a man like Kendrick wasn't the frightening part. The scary part was the act of being in love and what that represented. *It's scary because what if he doesn't love you back?* It was obvious that he cared for her, but love? Love had the ability to strengthen or damage relationships, and there was a very strong possibility that telling Kendrick that she wanted to stay in LA to see where their relationship would go was enough to send him running in the other direction.

True, she'd known that if given the chance, she'd stay in LA anyway to pursue her career and discuss with her colleagues the possibility of keeping the pop-up shop open longer, but Kendrick had been through hell and back with women from his past. He had every right to be apprehensive. *But you don't even know if he'll be apprehensive. What if he's receptive to the idea?*

As Kendrick continued to stroke her into a powerful

orgasm, the truth behind her fear had finally reared its ugly head. She wasn't just afraid of telling Kendrick how she felt because she was worried that he didn't feel the same way. She was afraid of telling Kendrick how she felt and realizing that he felt the exact same way. If that was the case, she'd have to own up to the fact that despite all her growth, the only thing she found more terrifying than allowing herself to fall in love was allowing herself to fall in love with the person who could be her future. That took courage... Courage that she wasn't sure she had.

Chapter 16

"I'll call you later," Kendrick said as he placed a kiss on Nicole's cheek.

"I look forward to it," Nicole said as she unlocked the door to the apartment. After having Nicole at his place all night and all morning, he didn't want her to leave. However, they both had to be at the studio tomorrow, and Nicole had to work at Bare Sophistication tonight. Since their jobs couldn't care less that they'd much rather stay in bed together the entire day, they chose to be responsible and see one another after work tomorrow.

Last night, he'd accepted what he'd known in his heart weeks before. He'd fallen completely in love with Nicole LeBlanc. Kendrick felt like he was floating on cloud nine as he walked back to his car. The moment he pulled out of the parking lot, his phone rang from a number he didn't recognize.

"This is Kendrick," he said when he answered.

"Kendrick? Is that you, baby?"

He pulled his car off to the shoulder at the sound of a voice he hadn't heard in two years. "Amanda, is that you?"

"Of course, it is, silly. Has it been that long?"

"Over two years," he said as a matter-of-factly.

"Two years? It only feels like two months to me. Listen, I need you to meet with me in an hour."

"No," he said. "You can't call out the blue and tell me to meet you somewhere."

"I see. You need me to be polite," she said with a forced laugh. "Kendrick, will you please meet with me in an hour?"

"No," he said again. "I'm busy."

"Busy," she said. "You mean with that woman I saw you walk out of your condo building with today?"

Kendrick frowned. "You don't know what you're talking about. You don't even know where I live."

"Yes, I do," she said. "You've lived a few blocks from the Third Street Promenade in Santa Monica for the past couple years. Just this morning you were wearing a burgundy tee and a pair of jeans. And I can't remember what that chick you were with was wearing, but trust me, I saw you. And I think it's best if you take me up on my offer to meet."

Kendrick dropped his head to his steering wheel. He'd known Amanda long enough to know that if he didn't oblige, it would only make matters worse.

"Where do you want to meet?"

"At the park we used to always go to."

"Okay, I'll be there in thirty minutes."

"I said an hour."

"Thirty minutes. I'll see you there." He disconnected the call and started driving in the direction of the park. His mind was racing with what she could possibly want. One thing he knew for sure. When Amanda popped up out the blue, it was never a good thing.

Kendrick glanced down at his watch. *Late as usual.* He'd told her to be here in thirty minutes, but she'd wanted to meet in an hour. Now it was an hour and a half since they talked, and she was just now strolling toward him.

"You're late," he said.

"I know," she said, flicking her hair over her shoulder. "Since you wanted me to be here in thirty minutes, I figured I'd make you wait it out."

Typical. She still enjoyed playing games. "Okay, so I'm here. What did you want to talk to me about?"

"Well, I'm not giving up on my acting, but I've decided that I would be a great set designer. Since I got out of rehab, I've worked on a few sets for community service work, and I loved it." She pulled out her résumé and handed it to him. "I need you to get your agency to sign me and tell them that I come highly recommended."

Kendrick grabbed the paper and read a few of her recommendations. "Are these recommendations legit?"

She cleared her throat, cracked her neck, then cleared her throat again. "Of course they are, silly."

She's lying. She always cleared her throat and cracked her neck when she was lying. "Amanda, I'm not convincing my agency to hire you."

"Why not?"

"Well, for starters, they are one of the most reputable agencies in LA."

"I know. That's why I want them to sign me."

"That also means that they have a no-bullshit mentality. You checked yourself back into rehab last year. How long have you been out?"

"For a month."

"How long have you been clean?"

"For a month. What does it matter?"

"It matters because I think you need to focus on getting healthy first."

"I am healthy," she said. "And I'm trying to get back my life, which is why I need you to talk to your agency."

Kendrick handed back her résumé. "I wish you the best, but I don't want to get involved. And I really think you need to focus on getting better first."

"What the fuck do you know?" she said as she stuffed the résumé back in her purse. It was then that Kendrick saw the bottle of liquor sticking out. He reached for it and pulled it out before taking a whiff of her breath.

"I thought you said you were clean?"

She grabbed the bottle from his hand and threw it back in her purse. "Who the hell are you to judge me?"

"I'm not judging you. I just want you to get better and realize that addiction is a disease, which means that you have to get the help you need." He stepped closer to her and lightly grabbed her elbow. "Amanda, don't you see that this path you're headed down is not a healthy one? You have to get the right help."

"Don't touch me," she yelled as she pulled her elbow away from him. "All my life, you've always looked down on me and thought you were better than me."

"That's not true."

"Yes, it is. And you and your self-righteousness are getting on my last nerve. I asked you to get me a job with your agency, and you pretty much laughed in my face. I didn't want to have to do this," she said. "I didn't want to go there."

"Do what?" he asked. "Go where?"

"I do have some connections in the industry," she says. "So if you can't get me the career I deserve, then I'll find someone who can."

"Amanda, you sound crazy right now."

"Do I?" she yelled. "Do I sound fucking crazy? How about now?" She raised her voice even more. "Embarrassed to be in public with me yet, or is that big-ass ego of yours too good to be embarrassed?" She took two steps closer to him. "After I leave this park, I want you to remember this as the day that I finally stopped letting your judgmental attitude affect me and took matters into my own hands. Just remember that I warned your ass before I exposed you."

He frowned. "What are you talking about?"

She laughed. "Don't you get it? I'm the only person

in this new life that you've created for yourself who knows the real you. The you behind that do-gooder image you try to portray. But just in case you need a reminder, how about I give you a hint." She got closer to his ear. "Ménage à trois." With that, she turned and stomped through the park the same way she came.

Crap. Crap. Crap. Crap. As much as Kendrick wanted to ignore Amanda's threat, he could tell that she was unhinged, so he wouldn't put anything past her. He pulled out his phone and called his uncle.

"Hey, nephew," Benjamin said. "What's up?"

Kendrick huffed. "I need to get ahold of your lawyer. Amanda is threating to expose my past."

"Expose your past how?" he asked.

"She has some pictures from a time in my life when I was at an all-time low. When I refused to help her get ahead in her career, she threatened to leak the pictures. I think she's desperate to get her fame one way or another." Kendrick ran his fingers down his face. "There may even be a video too."

"A video? Nephew, I think you better start at the beginning."

Kendrick grew more and more angry as he recounted the details to his uncle. By the end of his story, damaging his career wasn't the only worry he had. His relationship with Nicole would be in jeopardy, as well.

Nicole walked into the studio anxious to see Kendrick. She'd tried to contact him several times yesterday, and he hadn't responded to any of her calls or text messages. She'd had a strange feeling all morning, yet she couldn't really place it.

"Hey, sweetie," Angelica said as she gripped her arm. *She seems nervous.*

"Hey, Angelica. Is everything okay?"

"Of course it is. Why wouldn't it be? Have you seen Kendrick? Or have you talked to him today?"

"No." Nicole gave her a skeptical look. "Why do you ask? And why are you so nervous?" It was then that she noticed that everyone was staring at her with looks of pity.

"Um, why is everyone looking at me?"

Angelica nodded for Monty to come over. Once he reached them, Angelica and Monty took her into a small meeting room and shut the door.

"Listen," Monty said. "Kendrick is a good man. Please wait and talk to him about this before you draw your own conclusions."

"What are you talking about?" Nicole asked. "You guys are scaring me."

"It's pretty bad," Angelica said. "But I figured you'd rather see it with us than anyone else in the studio."

"Show me whatever it is that you're talking about," Nicole said. "I don't like the energy in this place right now."

Angelica and Monty shared a worried look before Monty took out his phone. "A popular blog site posted this today, so of course everyone who follows the blog got the notifications in their emails. Kendrick isn't famous or anything, but since he works in the film industry and through the agency, we have a lot of high-profile clients. News is spreading like wildfire."

Nicole took Monty's phone and pressed play on a video. Within the first few seconds, her mouth dropped. Kendrick was in the room with two other men and six females. She immediately recognized Amanda as one of the females. They are sitting around a table sniffing what she assumed was cocaine, drinking and shooting what she assumed was heroine. Although she wasn't sure what the drugs were and Kendrick only appeared to be drinking, it looked bad. It looked really bad.

"He looks young," Nicole said.

"Yeah," Monty said. "I don't know what's worse. If he was an adult or that he's obviously underage."

"People do crap way worse than this every day," Nicole said.

"Um, keep watching," Angelica said. A few minutes later, Nicole wished she'd stopped it just at the drugs and drinking, because watching Kendrick and Amanda have wild sex in a porno-style video before the whole room erupting into a sex frenzy was more than her stomach could handle at the moment.

"Oh, my God," Nicole said as she tried to hold down her breakfast. A part of her was completely shocked by what she was watching. However, another part of her felt so bad for Kendrick.

"Who leaked this?" Nicole asked. There was no way Kendrick had wanted this getting out into the world. *That's probably why he hasn't called me back.*

"I was only able to talk to Kendrick briefly when

he called this morning and asked me to make sure you were okay, but I think Amanda leaked it."

"I figured," Nicole said, handing Monty back his phone when Kendrick started throwing money at what she assumed to be strippers. She'd seen enough. "Why didn't he just ask me if I was okay himself?"

"He probably doesn't know what to say to you," Angelica said. "The Kendrick in this video is nothing like the man he is today. Up until you, Kendrick wasn't even a PDA type of guy. I know you probably have a lot of questions and he owes you a lot of answers, but give him time. My guess is, he's getting his lawyers on this right away."

"He is," Monty confirmed. "That's why he won't be at the studio today. And I can only imagine how the agency is handling this. We may work behind the scenes, but The Gilbert Monroe Agency lands some of the largest clients in the world by offering them the best, drama-free film crew that they could ask for. They once let go of the lead technician because his friend had gone live on Facebook when they were hiring prostitutes."

Nicole shook her head. "My heart is hurting for Kendrick." She pulled out her phone and tried to call him again. Still, no answer.

"Give him time," Angelica said. "And I'm sure if you can't handle being here today, the producers will let you go home and bring in one of the temp makeup artists."

"No," Nicole said as she composed herself to step out the meeting room. "Although I still need to process what I saw, I will not run out of here like an embarrassed little bunny."

"That's the spirit," Monty said. "Stand up for your man." Both Nicole and Angelica turned to face Monty. "Too much?"

"Just a little." She opened the door and as suspected, there was a small crowd gathered around the meeting room waiting for her to come out. *So many eyes*, she thought as she looked around the room. The old Nicole would have hung her head and tried to be invisible as she made her way through the crowd. However, the new Nicole was done hiding.

"Seriously, guys," she said to the room. "Don't act like that video is any worse than what most of you masturbate to on a daily basis. Next time I talk to Kendrick, I'll let him know that he provided endless entertainment and jokes all day."

Everyone laughed and the tension was broken. Nicole knew that it was only temporary and that Kendrick would probably be the main gossip all day, but she hoped that people would stop giving her those puppy-dog eyes.

"You're my shero," Angelica said as they walked through the crowd.

"That was badass," Monty said.

Nicole plastered on a smile, when internally she was so frustrated she wanted to scream at the top of her lungs. She glanced at her phone again, hoping she at least had a text message, but she didn't have anything.

Kendrick Burrstone, you have A LOT of explaining to do.

Chapter 17

"You have to call her, man," Monty said on the phone. "It's been two days, and the rumor around the studio is because Nicole was dating you, the agency decided not to extend her contract after today."

Kendrick could feel the blood rush from his face. "Please tell me you're joking."

"I wish I was, man, but Angelica was talking to her earlier, and it seems as if it's true. She seems to be holding up okay, but I shouldn't be the one giving her updates. You should be."

Kendrick had been going back and forth with the lawyers for the past couple days, trying to get the video taken down. Unfortunately, since Amanda owned the video, she had every right to leak it. They were confident that they would get it removed, but it would take longer than expected and everyone knew that the internet always remembered.

He'd just gotten off the phone with his mom, who'd suggested that he just own up to it, accept that it was out there and deal with the consequences. He knew she was right, and even though the lawyers were trying all different angles, the only thing that had been accomplished so far was him getting a restraining order on Amanda and her parents deciding to step in and get her the help she needed. It wouldn't be easy for her, but she was no longer his problem.

"I know, man. I want to talk to her, but I don't know what to say."

"What do you mean you don't know what to say?" Monty said. "Tell her that you messed up. Apologize. Beg for forgiveness. And praise her for standing tall amid all your BS. There aren't too many women who could handle the situation with style and grace like Nicole is. We're all disappointed that the agency isn't signing her on."

"You're right. I'll contact her and ask her if we could meet at her place tonight. There have been a few random media folks staked outside my place."

"Sounds good." Kendrick disconnected his call with Monty and called Nicole. She answered on the fourth ring.

Her sultry voice filled the line. "Hello?"

I forgot how much I missed this voice. "Hi, Nicole, it's Kendrick."

"I know," she said. "I was waiting for you to call."

"I'm sorry it took so long. I owe you an explanation,

and I was wondering if I could stop by your place tonight so that we could talk?"

She was silent for a few seconds before responding. "Sure, I'm free to talk tonight. Does seven work for you?"

"Yes, that works. I'll see you then." After he hung up the phone, his heart rate turned to normal. *You ruined her career in the industry.* He tried to shake the thought from his head, but he knew it was no use. He'd been thinking it ever since Monty told him that the agency wasn't going to hire her permanently. He had a meeting with the agency tomorrow morning, and he was pretty sure he knew how that meeting would go.

His uncle called, interrupting his thoughts. "Hey, Unc."

"Hey, so I'm calling because I had my financial adviser look into your finances, and everything looks good. It will be hard work, but if you want to do this, I think you should hit the ground with both feet."

Kendrick gave a sigh of relief. "Thanks, Unc. That's the best news I've gotten all week."

"I know," he said. "But remember that those who love and care about you will love you regardless of that video going public or not. We all make mistakes, but mistakes build character. You don't want to know what I was doing at that age, but that's a conversation for another day."

"I look forward to it," Kendrick said. "And thanks for all your help."

"Anytime, nephew."

As Kendrick disconnected the call, his mind drifted

back to Nicole. When he'd first met her, he was worried about dating someone who he worked with and it damaging his career. Little did he know, he'd managed to do that all by himself.

Nicole was a nervous wreck as she waited for Kendrick to arrive. When he'd called, her heart melted at the sound of his voice. She missed him so much, and she couldn't believe that after everything that had happened, this was her first time seeing him.

"Are you sure you don't want me to stay?" Kyra asked. "I don't mind."

"I'm sure," Nicole said. "We need to have a private conversation about everything."

"I understand. If you need me, I'll be around, so give me a call."

"Will do."

Once she was alone in the apartment, she took a deep breath. *You'll be fine. You've had a lot of time to process the video.* On the day that the video had been released, photos had been released later. When she thought about the entire situation, it almost seemed like she was watching someone else go through it, not her.

She jumped when she heard the knock on her door. When she opened it and saw him standing there, she had to do what she'd wanted to do for the past few days.

She leaped into his arms, pulling him into her embrace. He caught her and lifted her off the ground. When his lips found hers, she kissed him with all the built-up passion she had.

"Hi," she said when he'd lowered her to the ground.

"Hey back atcha." He placed one more quick kiss on her mouth before walking into her apartment.

Nicole motioned for them to sit on the couch. There was a nervous energy in the room, and she assumed that neither was too thrilled to have this conversation.

"I guess I should just get to it," Kendrick said. "First, I want to apologize for any of the pain and embarrassment that video may have caused. After I dropped you off four days ago, I got a call from Amanda saying that she wanted to meet. I told her no, but in the end, I knew she wouldn't leave me alone unless I saw her face-to-face.

"When I met with her, she told me that she needed me to get her hired by the agency so that she could jump-start her acting career. When I told her no and asked that she go back to rehab and take care of herself, she snapped. By the end of the conversation, she was threatening to make a move that would jeopardize my career."

"Based off what you're saying," Nicole said, "she must have had her contact release the video the next day?"

"Yes, she did. That next morning it was flooding the internet. And I know I should have called you right away and told you about everything that was happening, but I was part shocked. Part pissed. And part doing damage control."

"You still should have called me," Nicole said. "Do you know what it was like walking into the studio and having everyone know what's going on except for me?

Although I know you're going through a lot, it was the worst type of attention."

"I know it was." He lifted her hand in his. "And there is no excuse for how I handled this with you. When I didn't call you that first day, I think I pushed it off even more because I was scared to talk to you."

"Why?" she asked. "After all the serious conversations we had, why were you nervous to talk to me?"

"Because somewhere through the course of our friendship and then us dating, my feelings for you deepened in a way I've never felt with anyone before. To know that my past was exposed in such a damaging way was a lot to handle. But knowing that I could possibly lose you to this nonsense was even more nerve-racking."

"Kendrick, I'm not some precious doll who can't handle it when times get hard. Am I pissed that Amanda released that video? Yes. Do I hate that thousands of people got to see you naked and possibly even saved the video for their own personal collection? Absolutely. Am I upset that you didn't call me until days later? You better believe it. But never—despite the fact that we weren't working through this together— did I think about abandoning you. I'm not that type of person."

"I know you aren't," he said. "Nicole, you are everything I ever wanted for my future, and I was so caught up in trying not to have any repeat relationships like I had in the past that it never occurred to me that I'd be the one who caused you to lose out on an amazing career opportunity."

"The agency can kiss my ass," Nicole said. "I know that video was a lot to handle and any company would be freaking out, but to not extend a permanent contract to me because you and I date is completely ridiculous. So, I don't need to work for a company like that. I appreciate the opportunity I had because I learned about the film industry, and had it not been for the agency, I wouldn't have met you, Monty or Angelica."

Nicole adjusted herself on the couch so that she was facing him more. "And a silver lining did happen. I actually got an offer to work on two commercials being filmed in Miami. They contacted me earlier today."

His eyes widened. "That's great, Nicole. I'm so proud of you. I know you'll do great in Miami."

Huh? Was that a brush-off? "Yeah, I'm sure I will too. And speaking of Miami, I was actually hoping we could talk some more about it. You know filming ended today for the commercials and documentary, so I'm not in LA for that much longer."

"I know," he said. "That's another reason I wanted to see you today. I wasn't sure when you were going to head back home, so I wanted to make sure I cleared the air."

Yup, definitely a brush-off. "So that's the only reason you came over when you did? Would you have even come over to clear the air if I wasn't leaving?"

Nicole was fed up, and although she had hoped that her conversation with Kendrick would give her clarity on their relationship, proving that she should stay in LA and work it out, the conversation was managing to do the complete opposite.

"That's not the only reason," he said. "Yeah, it was a big reason I came over when I did, but it's because I couldn't leave things that way."

Nicole wasn't sure what had come over her, but her tolerance level was finally running on empty. She opened her mouth to give Kendrick a piece of her mind when his phone rang.

"I'm sorry, I've been waiting on that call. Give me one second." He walked into the kitchen to take the call, leaving a fuming Nicole on the couch. A few minutes later, he returned. "I hate to do this, but I have to go. You know I wouldn't leave if it wasn't important. Can I call you tomorrow so we can set up another time to meet?"

Seriously! "Yeah, sure." With that, he kissed her cheek and walked out the door. Twenty minutes later, Nicole was still in disbelief at how terrible that conversation had gone, so she called her favorite person in the world.

Her grandmother answered on the first ring. "Hey, sweet pea. Are you okay?"

Nicole had told her grandma what had transpired, however, when Gran had asked her what she was going to do about Kendrick, she'd told her she had to wait until after she'd spoken to him.

"No, I'm not okay," she said. "Kendrick just came over, and basically, it doesn't seem like he wants to continue our relationship."

"Sweet pea, did he say those exact words?"

"No, he didn't. But he implied them. Everything he said implied them."

"Did you flat out ask him if he wanted to continue dating?"

"Of course not, Gran," Nicole said. "I had to maintain some bit of dignity."

"Well, if you didn't ask him, then you really don't know how he feels, now do you?"

"I know that if he cared about me like I cared about him, he wouldn't have left my apartment tonight without me being absolutely certain on where we stood."

"I understand that, sweet pea, but men are different creatures. They don't think the same way we do. They don't process things the same way we do. So whenever you say to yourself that it's the way you would have handled the situation, remind yourself that men are not the same as women."

Nicole sat back on the couch and let her grandmother's words sink in. "I don't know, maybe you're right. Maybe I just need a break."

"Listen, why don't you come home for a few days? I know you have some stuff in the works in LA, but why don't you come home and clear your mind?"

Nicole smiled. A visit with Gran would do her some good. "I'd like that, Gran," she said. "And I think I need this trip ASAP. I'll book a flight that leaves tomorrow."

"Sounds good," Gran said. "I can't wait to see my sweet pea."

"I can't wait to see you either, Gran." Nicole disconnected the call feeling a lot better about the situation than she had before. *Maybe Gran is right. When I get back to LA, I'll finally just tell Kendrick how I feel and be honest.*

Chapter 18

"She's where?" Kendrick asked for the third time.

"How many times do I have to tell you?" Kyra said to Kendrick, who was standing in the doorway of the apartment. "Based off your last conversation, she said she could tell that you didn't love her, so she moved back to Miami. She said there was nothing left for her in LA."

"So she just left without saying goodbye? That makes no sense."

Kyra frowned. "I guess it makes about as much sense as a video leaking on the internet and instead of talking it out with his girlfriend, the star ignores her."

"Point taken," he said. "Do you at least have her address in Miami?"

"Why?" Kyra asked. "Do you plan on flying down

there and telling her that you love her and you're an idiot?"

"Yes," he said. "Probably in that exact order."

Kyra quirked an eyebrow. "How do I know that you aren't just saying that so that I'll give you her address?"

Kendrick sighed. "Although I really want to express these feelings to Nicole first, I can tell you I am completely and irrevocably in love with her. She's not just my present. She's my future, and right now, all I can think about doing is hopping on a plane to see her and either convince her to stay in LA or tell her I'm willing to move to Miami."

"Seriously?" Kyra asked. "You'd move to Miami?"

"I'd move to Timbuktu if that meant I'd have the chance to be with her forever."

A smile slowly crept on Kyra's face. "Congratulations, lover boy. You've passed the test."

Kyra wrote the address on a piece of paper and handed it to him. "Don't make me regret this."

"I won't," he said as he rushed down the hall. It was time for him to go get his woman.

"How you doing, sweet pea?"

Nicole turned to face Gran. "I'm doing okay. I missed this view." Gran's house sat right near the ocean, and one of Nicole's favorite things to do was to sit in one of the beach chairs and just stare out into the water.

Gran sat down on the chair next to her. "There's something I've been meaning to talk to you about."

"What is it?" Nicole asked.

"It's about your mother."

"Gran," Nicole said, "it's been a rough few days. Do we have to talk about her today?"

"We do," Gran said. "I probably should have told you this years ago, but after your father walked out on your mother, she was devastated and didn't know how to handle the fact that her marriage was ending."

"No, she wasn't," Nicole said. "She didn't seem fazed at all when my dad left. In fact, to me, she acted as if a burden was lifted from her shoulders with him gone and me living with you and Grandpa."

"It wasn't. Your mom doesn't process things like the average person. But trust me, she didn't take it well. And I know it's been years since you've seen your mom, which is why I feel like it's my duty to explain to you that you need to let go of the part of your heart that secretly holds on to the idea that she will pop up one day and be the mother you've always wanted."

"I don't hold on to that fairy tale."

"Yes, you do," Gran said. "And even though it's fine to hold on to a fairy tale every now and then, when it comes to your mother, she never had the nurturing qualities of the everyday mother, but she's always loved you. She just doesn't know how to show it."

"She doesn't show it at all," Nicole said.

Gran gently tapped her hand. "I know, sweet pea. Your mom is good at being a lieutenant in the army. That's what she's good at. And I don't want to frustrate you by bringing up your mother, but there will come a time when I won't be here, and I need to know that you don't have a heavy heart because of things that you can't change, and won't be afraid to take chances because you're harboring what's happened to you in the past."

Nicole knew what Gran was trying to say, and even though she didn't want to ever think about a time when Gran wasn't here, she was right. She needed to forgive her mother so that she could release any ill will she was holding toward her and move on from that relationship. Certain women just weren't meant to be mothers, and she knew Ruby Meech was one of them.

"I understand, Gran. And I promise that I won't carry around a heavy heart. It's going to take time, but I'm working on it." Nicole glanced at the time on her iPhone. "I have to get to Bare Sophistication for a couple photoshoots this afternoon, but I appreciate this talk and for all the talks you've ever had with me about life and how to live it to its fullest."

"Aww, you're welcome, sweet pea." Nicole leaned over and gave her a hug. "I'm going to miss these hugs when you're in LA."

"I'll be coming back and forth," Nicole said. "Kyra and I are really excited to find a permanent location for Bare Sophistication and to implement some of our ideas for that market. I already told you I landed those Miami commercials, so I'll be home then too."

"Good," Gran said, hugging her even tighter. "Gives me something to look forward to."

"You got this," Kendrick said to himself. It wasn't until he was on the plane headed to Miami that he realized Kyra had given him the address to the Bare

Sophistication location in Miami instead of Nicole's address like he'd asked for.

He supposed he deserved it based off how he'd handled the situation with the video leak. He'd gone over his speech in his head several times, but as he approached the shop, he suddenly couldn't remember anything.

"Are going to walk up and down the street all day?"

Kendrick turned to face the voice. "Aaliyah, hey."

"Hey, yourself," she said with a laugh. "Kyra called me a few hours ago and said you'd probably show up. And apparently, I'm supposed to help you locate Nicole."

Kendrick frowned. "You mean, she's not in the boutique?"

Aaliyah squinted her eyes. "Maybe, maybe not. Why should I tell you?"

He smiled at the fact that she interrogated him just as Kyra had done. He liked that Nicole had such protective friends. "Because Nicole is my future and all I can think about doing right now is expressing that love and hoping like hell she feels the same way. If she wants to stay here in Miami, I'll move here with her if that's what it takes. I just can't go another minute without telling her how I feel. She deserves to know that she's completely stolen my heart."

Aaliyah's heart clenched. "That was beautiful. Okay then," she said, clasping her hands together. "Follow me."

The moment Kendrick stepped into the shop, he was greeted by two women.

"Hello, Kendrick," said the pregnant one. "My name is Summer."

"And I'm Danni," the other woman said as she reached out her hand. Kendrick briefly noticed the sparkling diamond on her ring finger that he assumed was an engagement ring. "And I'll have you know that if you break Nicole's heart, you won't just have Gran to answer to but a host of people ready to put you in your place."

"Noted," he said to both of the women. "But you don't have to worry about that. I'll never hurt her, and all I can do is apologize for the hurt I've already caused."

All three women seemed to be sizing him up. It was Summer who spoke next. "I guess it's only fair that we also tell you that we contacted your cousins back in Chicago because we happen to be close with the founders of Elite Events Incorporated, and they agreed with us. If another video or photo of you is ever released, the first person you need to contact is Nicole."

"That's right," Danni said. "A happy home starts with good communication. Take it from someone who learned the hard way, being honest and open is always better than keeping secrets."

Kendrick nodded in agreement. "I agree, and I promise that you, my cousins and Gran have nothing to worry about." He glanced around the shop. "I don't want to be rude, but there is a woman I'm dying to see and apologize to. Do you know where she is?"

Danni smiled. "She's upstairs."

"Follow me," Aaliyah said again. Kendrick trailed

Aaliyah up a set of stairs to an area that looked similar to the Bare Sophistication boudoir studio he'd seen in the California pop-up.

When they turned the corner, Nicole's back was to them, as she was doing someone's makeup. *Finally, there she is.* He'd known he'd been anxious to see her. He just hadn't known how much until he finally laid eyes on her.

"Nicole," Aaliyah said. "There's someone here to see you."

"Okay, I'm finishing up my current client now. Is my five o'clock early?"

Kendrick cleared his throat. "Um, no. It's not your five o'clock. And I wouldn't say I'm too early. It's more like I'm hoping I'm not too late."

Nicole froze as she slowly turned around to face him. "What are you doing here?" she asked.

"When I went back to your apartment early this morning, Kyra told me that you'd decided to come back to Miami, and I realized that once again I'd handled our conversation poorly since I'd left pretty abruptly last night and didn't explain why."

Nicole squinted her eyes. "You didn't want to just wait until I returned to LA to talk?"

Kendrick's eyes flew to Aaliyah as he laughed to himself. "Uh, no, I couldn't wait until you got back to LA."

Nicole placed her arms over her chest. "Kyra told you that I'd moved back permanently, didn't see?" She glanced at Aaliyah. "And I'm assuming Aaliyah didn't correct you when you saw her before she brought you up here?"

"It doesn't matter," Kendrick said, stepping closer to her. "Because what I need to say, it doesn't matter whether you're living here or in LA. If you want to stay here, I'd work something out. I just want to be with you."

Nicole's eyes widened. "What do you mean?"

Kendrick held his hands out in front of him. "Wait, let me start over."

"How about I bring your client back in a half hour?" Aaliyah said, helping the customer out the chair. "Miss, how about you pick out any lingerie set you want in our boutique. Compliments of the shop."

"Oh, I'd like that," the woman said. "And good luck." She flashed Kendrick two thumbs-up.

Once they were alone, Kendrick grabbed both of Nicole's hands. "I wanted to start off by apologizing again. Last night, I handled that conversation completely wrong, and it wasn't until I was halfway to my meeting that I realized that I'd forgotten to tell you some of the most important things that I'd wanted to tell you."

She studied his eyes. "Which are?"

"Well, before everything happened, I was falling madly in love with you. After that video leaked, instead of turning your back on me, you tried your best to be there for me in any way you could. Although I didn't handle your support the right way, it made my love for you grow stronger than it already was. Nicole, you're it for me. You're the reason I want to wake up in the morning and the reason I go to bed with a smile. You challenge me. You inspire me. I could literally spend all day listening to you talk because I'm that intrigued by this mouth of yours.

"If someone would have told me that the way I'd find my one true love was when she spilled drinks all over me at a bar, I wouldn't have believed them. Especially if they'd also said I'd fall for someone I work with. But that's exactly what happened with you. I love you and I fell so hard so fast that I wasn't even sure if you were ready to learn my true feelings."

"I was," she said, squeezing his hands tighter. "I started falling for you early too, although I tried to deny it at first. We've both been burned badly before, so you know how hard it is to open up your heart to love when everything from your past has tried to prove that true love wasn't in the cards for you. But now I see that it wasn't the case. True love doesn't care about what's happened in the past. True love doesn't care about how many times your heart was broken, but rather, how many times you're willing to lay your heart on the line."

Nicole took a deep breath. "Kendrick, I love you too, and I have for a while. Every time I decided to tell you, I'd lose my nerve. But loving you is one of the easiest things I've ever done in my life. You understand me. You make me feel beautiful. You listen when I talk, and any time spent with you is time well spent."

Kendrick pulled her to him, his lips crashing on hers in a frenzied kiss that released all the emotions and tension they'd tried their best to hide.

"So, what do we do now?" Nicole asked when they took a moment to breathe.

"Well, I also wanted to tell you that whether you live in LA or Miami, my heart and home are with you, so I'm willing to move if that's what you want."

"No need," Nicole said with a laugh. "We had a conference call several days ago about the Bare Sophistication pop-up in LA because it's doing so well. For at least another year, Kyra and I—and the employees we hired—are going to spend the time building up the location and revenue. Paperwork was signed a couple days ago. And although it was going to be hard to be in the same city as the man I loved and not have him reciprocate that love, this is soooo much better."

Kendrick smiled. "I agree. I have some news too. It's going to take a lot of hard work, but I've met with several financial and business providers, and I have the funds to start my own production company."

"That's so amazing," Nicole said as she gave him a hug. "I'm so proud of you."

"Thanks, baby." He dipped his head in the curve of her neck. "Do you have time to step away for a quick glass of champagne to celebrate? I noticed it's happy hour at a place down the street."

"I should have at least another twenty minutes before Aaliyah brings back my client. Let me grab my purse and we can sneak out the back door."

"Sounds like a plan." He waited until she'd escaped to a room that he assumed her purse was in before he made his next move.

"Oh, my…" Her words trailed off when she stepped

out of the room and noticed that Kendrick was down on one knee displaying a gorgeous diamond ring.

"Nicole, there is so much about you that I love that I'm not even sure where to start. I've never met anyone who challenged me the way you do, forcing me to not only define the person I wanted to be, but to acknowledge the person I was in the past. I know you've had to endure more than most, but I think all of the obstacles you've faced in life are what made you the wonderful woman you are today. I could spend the rest of my life telling you that I love you every day, and even that wouldn't be enough to truly express all the love I have in my heart.

"So right here, right now, I'm asking you to not only be my wife, but to be my partner... My best friend... My confidante... My support. And in exchange, I swear to be all of those to you and to always make sure you feel cherished and loved. When we first met, we knew we'd been placed in each other's life for a reason, but neither of us had any idea that cupid had shot his last arrow at us. And as unexpected as our love was, I will forever be grateful for it. Nicole, will you marry me?"

She nodded as she wiped the tears that had fallen on her cheeks. "Yes," she said through her sobs. "I'll marry you, Kendrick."

Placing the ring on her finger, he picked her up and spun her around the room. The cheers from the doorway proved that her friends and client had heard the proposal, as well.

"You know tomorrow is Valentine's Day," she said when her tears had subsided.

"You know what that means," he said.

She studied his eyes. "What does it mean?"

"It means for the first time in my life, I'm actually excited to celebrate that holiday."

She laughed as a few more tears escaped. He was sure he should put her down since he was holding her so close, but he couldn't let her go just yet. After all this time, he'd found his perfect match. He'd found the woman he would spend the rest of his life with. Sometimes, when life threw wrenches into your plans, it was hard to see the rainbow on the other side of a dark and stormy night. In some ways, he'd been through hell and back, but had managed to capture the love of a woman who not only forced him to view life differently, but to appreciate those differences in any and everything.

As Kendrick gazed into the eyes of the woman he loved, he was certain that life as he knew it would never be the same. With Nicole by his side, it would only be better.

Epilogue

Three months later...

"Are you happy?"

Nicole smiled at her fiancé. They were already an hour late to meet Kendrick's mom to discuss wedding plans, but Felicia Burrstone was getting used to it. Nicole and Kendrick may be a lot of things, but on time they were not. "Yes, baby, I'm happy. Are you going to ask me that every day?"

"Not every day," he said. "But probably every day until we get married. Maybe even a little after."

She laughed. It had been only three months, but it had been the best three months of her life. Sales at Bare Sophistication in LA had taken off once they moved into a permanent location. Aaliyah still flew in at least once a month to work at the boutique and boudoir studio as well as visit her aunt.

The founders of Bare Sophistication each had husbands with offices in LA, so she often saw all her friends. Of course, since two of her brothers were married to founders, that meant Kyra saw them a lot more than she'd wanted and always felt like they were checking up on her, but all in all, she could tell that Kyra loved how often her family visited.

The best news of all had been when the lawyers called to say that the video and all discriminating photos of Kendrick had been removed from the blog site, even though they knew the internet never forgot. Kendrick had used the situation as a platform to speak to the younger generation, in particular young men who were in the same predicament he'd been in. Kendrick's story about how he turned his life around had gotten the attention of many. Not long after news about him starting his own production company began to circulate, he'd been hired by twelve companies who wanted him and his staff to produce their commercials. Of course, Bare Sophistication, Burrstone Winery and Distillery and Elite Events Incorporated were at the top of the list!

True to their character, Monty and Angelica hadn't liked the way that The Gilbert Monroe Agency had treated Kendrick and Nicole, so once Kendrick got his company off the ground, they were more than eager to quit despite the fact that Kendrick had told them that it wasn't necessary. Nicole had to remind him that when God handed you blessings, the last thing you did was push them away. So he'd accepted them on the staff and so far the four amigos were back in business.

Overall, life was looking pretty good, and Nicole couldn't ask for anything more. Kendrick had finished her tattoo, and it had turned out beautifully. Already, Kendrick was working on another design for her.

Gran and her boyfriend, Mike, were going to be visiting next month, and Nicole had even managed to Skype with her mom twice. The conversations had been short, but it was what Nicole had needed. At the end of both video calls, she'd told her mom that she loved her. Although Ruby Meech had yet to say it back, Nicole was confident that eventually her mom would open more. Like Gran always said, some people let fear keep them rooted in place, never expanding their branches and reaching their full potential. Gran even mentioned that Ruby had spent her entire life never expressing her love for anyone, but that didn't mean she didn't love Nicole. It just meant that she didn't know how to show it.

"Are you happy?" Nicole asked as they pulled up in front of his mom's house.

"Happier than I ever thought possible," he said, bringing her in for a kiss. As did all of their kisses, it quickly escalated.

They walked up the sidewalk to the house. When they got closer to the door, Nicole stopped walking.

"What's wrong?" Kendrick asked. "You look like you're going to be sick."

"That's a strong possibility," she said with a nervous laugh. "Can I ask you a question?"

"Um, sure," he said. "Are you sure everything is okay?"

"Everything is fine," she said. "I meant everything could be fine, but I'm not sure if it's fine yet. I mean, what does the word fine really mean? Is it another way to say that you're doing okay? Well, of course it is. You know what, never mind, let's go see your mom."

Kendrick blinked. "I can't believe it," he said as his eyes widened. "You're pregnant, aren't you?"

"What?" Nicole gasped. "How did you guess that?"

"You are, aren't you?" He rushed to her and cradled her face in his hands. "Please tell me, Nicole. Are you?"

"Yes, I am," she said with a smile. "I'm—"

"You're three months pregnant, right?"

"How are you guessing so accurately?" she said.

"Because I've suspected it for over a month," he said. "I just didn't want to get my hopes up."

"How have you known? We've been so busy that I didn't even notice that Aunt Flo hadn't come to visit. I only just found out last week."

"I knew because I know your body better than anyone," he said. "Your breasts were tender at times when we made love. Your skin has been glowing more than usual. And we haven't had to postpone lovemaking in a while because of Aunt Flo, so I knew it was a possibility." He pulled her closer to him. "I also remember how wild our night was in Miami the day I proposed, so I'm not surprised that we managed to make a baby."

She pulled him down to her for a kiss. *I am so in love with this man.* And now, they were going to have a baby together. It was perfect. Life was perfect.

"Are you two going to stand outside all day?" Felicia asked from her porch. The bright pink sundress and headband made Nicole smile. Her future mother-in-law had become one of her favorite people to talk to and hang out with.

"Hey, Mom." Kendrick kissed Felicia's cheek.

"Hey, Ms. Burrstone," Nicole said as she gave her a hug.

"Sweetie, soon you're going to have to start calling me Mom." Suddenly, Felicia stood back and looked Nicole up and down. "Oh. My. God."

"What?" Nicole said. "What is it?"

"You're pregnant," Felicia said. "Are you pregnant?"

"How do you both do that?" Nicole asked, looking from Kendrick to Felicia.

"So, you are?" Felicia asked. "Am I going to be a grandmother?"

"Yes, you are," Nicole said with a smile. "I just found out last week."

Felicia's hands flew to her face. "Ahhh," she screamed. "I'm going to be a grandmother. Ahhh, I can't believe it. I've got to call my siblings and tell all my friends."

By now, Felicia was pacing back and forth across the porch. "I don't believe this. I DON'T BELIEVE IT!" she yelled.

"Mom," Kendrick said as he tried to control his laughter. "Are you trying to tell the entire neighborhood."

"Yes, son. That's exactly what I'm trying to do. Ahh, I can't believe it."

Nicole was laughing so hard, tears were streaming down her cheeks.

"Come on inside, sweetie," Felicia said. "Wedding talk can wait until later. Instead, let's discuss baby names. Do you know if it's a boy or girl yet? I have some unisex names in mind that could work. You know you have to calm down your busy schedule, right? And are you eating healthy? Let me make you something. What do you want to eat?"

The questions were coming so fast, Nicole couldn't even respond.

"I'm sorry," Kendrick whispered. "My mom tends to go overboard when she's excited. But don't worry, I'll tell her that she can't name our future kid."

"Not yet," Nicole said with a smile. "I never had a mom this involved, so it's kinda nice to hear all the love and enthusiasm pouring from her voice."

"You mean all the crazy and overbearing things pouring from her mouth," Kendrick said with a laugh. "But you're right. My mom already loved you like a daughter, and after this news, she's probably so excited she can barely contain herself."

As Nicole stood back and watched Felicia continue to rattle off ideas she had for the nursey, she took the time to soak in the moment. When she'd decided to start her self-reflection journey a few years ago, she never would have predicted that her path would land her here, but that's exactly what happened. For someone who was once scared to live life on her own terms, she barely recognized that woman anymore.

Neither she nor Kendrick were perfect, but together,

they were invincible. She was no longer nervous about what the future would bring but instead was ready to tackle the unknown and make the most out of life.

* * * * *

KIMANI™
ROMANCE

COMING NEXT MONTH
Available February 20, 2018

#561 TO TEMPT A STALLION
The Stallions • by Deborah Fletcher Mello
Marketing guru Rebecca "Bec" Marks has had eyes for Nathaniel Stallion from day one. Regardless of Nathaniel's naïveté to her crush, her ardor for the newly crowned restaurateur remains intact. And when her romantic plans are threatened, she'll pull out all the stops to prove she's his soul mate…

#562 HIS SAN DIEGO SWEETHEART
Millionaire Moguls • by Yahrah St. John
Hotel manager Miranda Jensen needs to marry to inherit her grandfather's fortune. The treasurer of the San Diego Millionaire Moguls chapter, Vaughn Ellicott, offers her the perfect solution. Until she begins to fall for their pretend affair. Will Vaughn choose to turn their make-believe marriage into a passionate reality?

#563 EXCLUSIVELY YOURS
Miami Dreams • by Nadine Gonzalez
When Leila Amis meets her new boss, top Miami Realtor Nicolas Adrian, their explosive attraction culminates in a brief fling. Then their affair ends in bitter regrets, leaving Nick heartbroken. A year later, he's back with an irresistible offer. With even more at stake, can Nick make Leila his forever?

#564 SOMETHING ABOUT YOU
Coleman House • by Bridget Anderson
Pursuing her PhD while working at her cousin's bed-and-breakfast and organic farm leaves little personal time for Kyla Coleman. Until she meets Miles Parker. There's something about the baseball legend turned food industry entrepreneur that captivates her. When a business opportunity comes between them, can Miles persuade Kyla he's worthy of her trust?

Get 2 Free Books,
Plus 2 Free Gifts—
just for trying the Reader Service!

SPECIAL EXCERPT FROM

Plenty of women have tried to capture the treasurer of the San Diego chapter of the Millionaire Moguls, Vaughn Ellicott. When the ex-naval officer meets a gorgeous stranger in need of help, he surprises himself by offering her a mutually beneficial deal. Career-minded Vaughn tells himself that their business arrangement will get his family off his back. But suddenly that's not nearly as important as getting his beautiful new bride into bed...

Read on for a sneak peek at
HIS SAN DIEGO SWEETHEART,
the next exciting installment in the
***MILLIONAIRE MOGULS** continuity by Yahrah St. John!*

"Ahem." Miranda coughed loudly, bringing her right hand to her mouth.

He glanced up from his conversation, but didn't make any effort to speak. Instead his dark eyes gleamed like glassy volcanic rock as he boldly raked her from the top of her hair to her now aching feet. Pumps were definitely not made for all the walking she'd done today. "Are you done with your appraisal?" Miranda inquired. Flirting could work to her benefit if it garnered his interest. Though he would soon find out she had an agenda.

"Nearly." He continued to scan her critically for several more moments before he beamed his approval and looked her dead in the eye.

"And?"

A perplexed look crossed his features. "And what?"

"Do you like what you see?" Miranda inquired.

"Yes. Yes, I do very much."

Miranda's insides jangled with excitement as she slid onto the bar stool beside him. The bartender came to her immediately. "Have you decided if you'd like another?"

"Actually, I'd like something stronger." She turned to her companion. "What would you recommend?"

He grinned a delicious stomach-curling smile. "Max, get her a bourbon, same as me." He swiveled around to face her. "It's a bit strong, but I think you'll like it."

"I like strong," Miranda countered. "Men, that is."

"Is that a fact?"

She smiled coquettishly. "It is indeed. I noticed you earlier surfing." She inclined her head toward the beach that was about a hundred yards away.

"And did *you* like what you saw?"

She raised a brow. He'd seen her watching him, so she answered honestly. "You know I did. It was quite entertaining watching you out there."

"And afterward?"

An image of him in the wet suit flashed across Miranda's mind. "The view wasn't bad either."

Her stranger laughed heartily and Miranda liked the sound of it. It was deep and masculine and the very air around her seemed electrified being next to him.

"Well, aren't you a breath of fresh air. You actually say what's on your mind."

"Miranda." She extended her hand. "Miranda Jensen."

Don't miss HIS SAN DIEGO SWEETHEART
by Yahrah St. John, available March 2018
wherever Harlequin® Kimani Romance™
books and ebooks are sold!

*Savannah Carlisle infiltrated a Tennessee bourbon empire
for revenge, not to fall for the seductive heir of it all. But
as the potential for scandal builds and one little secret
exposes everything, will it cost her the love of a man she
was raised to hate?*

*Read on for a sneak peek at
SAVANNAH'S SECRETS
by Reese Ryan,
the first book in the **BOURBON BROTHERS** trilogy!*

Blake's attention snapped to the source of the voice.

His temperature climbed instantly when he encountered the woman's sly smile and hazel eyes sparkling in the sunlight.

Her dark, wavy hair was pulled into a low bun. If she'd worn the sensible gray suit to downplay her gorgeous features, it was a spectacular fail.

The woman extended her hand. "Please, call me Savannah."

Blake shook her hand and was struck by the contrast of her soft skin against his. Electricity sparked in his palm. He withdrew his hand and shoved it into his pocket.

"Miss…Savannah, please, have a seat." He indicated the chair opposite his desk.

She complied. One side of her mouth pulled into a slight grin, drawing his attention to her pink lips.

Were they as soft and luscious as they looked? He swallowed hard, fighting back his curiosity as to the flavor of her gloss.

Blake sank into the chair behind his desk, thankful for the solid expanse between them.

He was the one with the authority here. So why did it seem that she was assessing him?

Relax and stay focused.

He was behaving as if he hadn't seen a stunningly beautiful woman before.

"Tell me about yourself, Savannah."

It was a standard interview opening. But he genuinely wanted to learn everything there was to know about this woman.

Savannah crossed one long, lean leg over the other. Her skirt shifted higher, grazing the top of her knee and exposing more of her golden-brown skin. She was confident and matter-of-fact in talking about her accomplishments as an event planner.

She wasn't the first job candidate to gush about the company history in an attempt to ingratiate herself with him. But something in her eyes indicated deep admiration. Perhaps even reverence for what his family had built.

"You've done your homework, and you know our history." Blake sat back in his leather chair. "But my primary concern is what's still on the horizon. How will you impact the future of King's Finest?"

"Excellent question." Savannah produced a leather portfolio from her large tote. "One I'm prepared to answer. Give me two months and I'll turn the jubilee into a marketing bonanza that'll get distributors and consumers excited about your brand."

An ambitious claim, but an intriguing one.

"You have my attention, Savannah Carlisle." Blake crossed one ankle over his knee. "Wow me."